Bret Harte, Robert B Honeyman

Wan Lee

The Pagan

Bret Harte, Robert B Honeyman

Wan Lee
The Pagan

ISBN/EAN: 9783744652698

Printed in Europe, USA, Canada, Australia, Japan

Cover: Foto ©Raphael Reischuk / pixelio.de

More available books at **www.hansebooks.com**

Wan Lee, the Pagan

AND

OTHER SKETCHES

BY

BRET HARTE

LONDON

GEORGE ROUTLEDGE AND SONS

CONTENTS.

————◆◆————

WAN LEE, THE PAGAN.

AS I opened Hop Sing's letter, there fluttered to the ground a square strip of yellow paper covered with hieroglyphics, which, at first glance, I innocently took to be the label from a pack of Chinese fire-crackers. But the same envelope also contained a smaller strip of rice-paper, with two Chinese characters traced in Indian ink, that I at once knew to be Hop Sing's visiting-card. The whole, as afterwards literally translated, ran as follows :—

> " To the stranger the gates of my house are not
>   closed : the rice-jar is on the left, and the
>   sweetmeats on the right as you enter.
> Two sayings of the Master :—
>   Hospitality is the virtue of the son and the
>   wisdom of the ancestor.
>   The Superior man is light-hearted after the
>   crop-gathering : he makes a festival.
> When the stranger is in your melon-patch, observe him
>   not too closely : inattention is often the highest form
>   of civility.
>   Happiness, Peace, and Prosperity.
>   HOP SING."

Admirable, certainly, as was this morality and proverbial wisdom, and although this last axiom

was very characteristic of my friend Hop Sing,
who was that most sombre of all humourists, a
Chinese philosopher, I must confess that, even
after a very free translation, I was at a loss to
make any immediate application of the message.
Luckily I discovered a third enclosure in the shape
of a little note in English, and Hop Sing's own
commercial hand.   It ran thus :—

"The pleasure of your company is requested at No. —
Sacramento Street, on Friday evening at eight o'clock.
A cup of tea at nine,—sharp.

HOP SING."

This explained all.   It meant a visit to Hop
Sing's warehouse, the opening and exhibition of
some rare Chinese novelties and *curios*, a chat in
the back office, a cup of tea of a perfection
unknown beyond these sacred precincts, cigars,
and a visit to the Chinese theatre or temple.   This
was, in fact, the favorite programme of Hop Sing
when he exercised his functions of hospitality as
the chief factor or superintendent of the Ning Foo
Company.

At eight o'clock on Friday evening I entered
the warehouse of Hop Sing.   There was that
deliciously commingled mysterious foreign odour
that I had so often noticed : there was the old
array of uncouth-looking objects, the long pro-
cession of jars and crockery, the same singular
blending of the grotesque and the mathematically

neat and exact, the same endless suggestions of frivolity and fragility, the same want of harmony in colours that were each, in themselves, beautiful and rare. Kites in the shape of enormous dragons and gigantic butterflies; kites so ingeniously arranged as to utter at intervals, when facing the wind, the cry of a hawk; kites so large as to be beyond any boy's power of restraint—so large that you understood why kite-flying in China was an amusement for adults; gods of china and bronze so gratuitously ugly as to be beyond any human interest or sympathy from their very impossibility; jars of sweetmeats covered all over with moral sentiments from Confucius; hats that looked like baskets, and baskets that looked like hats; silks so light that I hesitate to record the incredible number of square yards that you might pass through the ring on your little finger :—these, and a great many other indescribable objects, were all familiar to me. I pushed my way through the dimly-lighted warehouse, until I reached the back office, or parlour, where I found Hop Sing waiting to receive me.

Before I describe him, I want the average reader to discharge from his mind any idea of a Chinaman that he may have gathered from the pantomime. He did not wear beautifully scalloped drawers, fringed with little bells (I never met a Chinaman who did); he did not habitually carry his fore-finger extended before him at right angles with his body; nor did I ever hear him utter the mysterious sentence, " Ching a ring a ring chaw ;" nor dance under any provocation. He was, on the whole, a rather grave, decorous, handsome gentleman. His complexion, which extended all over his head, except where his long pig-tail grew, was like a very nice piece of glazed brown paper-muslin. His eyes were black and bright, and his eyelids set at an angle of fifteen degrees ; his nose straight and delicately formed; his mouth small, and his teeth white and clean. He wore a dark blue silk blouse, and in the streets, on cold days, a jacket of astrachan fur. He wore, also, a pair of drawers of blue brocade gathered tightly over his calves and ankles, offering a general sort of suggestion that he had forgotten his trousers that morning, but that, so gentlemanly were his manners, his friends had forborne to mention the fact to him. His manner was urbane, although quite serious. He spoke French and English fluently. In brief, I doubt if you could have found the equal of this Pagan shopkeeper among the Christian traders of San Francisco.

There were a few others present—a judge of the Federal Court, an editor, a high government official, and a prominent merchant. After we had drunk our tea, and tasted a few sweetmeats from a mysterious jar, that looked as if it might contain a preserved mouse among its other nondescript treasures, Hop Sing arose, and, gravely beckoning

us to follow him, began to descend to the basement. When we got there, we were amazed at
finding it brilliantly lighted, and that a number of
chairs were arranged in a half-circle on the asphalte
pavement. When he had courteously seated us,
he said :

" I have invited you to witness a performance
which I can at least promise you no other foreigners but yourselves have ever seen. Wang, the
court-juggler, arrived here yesterday morning. He
has never given a performance outside of the palace
before. I have asked him to entertain my friends
this evening. He requires no theatre, stage acces-
sories, or any confederate—nothing more than you
see here. Will you be pleased to examine the
ground yourselves, gentlemen ? "

Of course we examined the premises. It was the
ordinary basement or cellar of the San Francisco
storehouse, cemented to keep out the damp. We
poked our sticks into the pavement, and rapped on
the walls to satisfy our polite host—but for no other
purpose. We were quite content to be the victims
of any clever deception. For myself, I knew I was
ready to be deluded to any extent, and, if I had
been offered an explanation of what followed, I
should probably have declined it.

Although I am satisfied that Wang's general
performance was the first of that kind ever given
on American soil, it has, probably, since become so
familiar to many of my readers that I shall not

bore them with it here. He began by setting to flight, with the aid of his fan, the usual number of butterflies, made before our eyes of little bits of tissue-paper, and kept them in the air during the remainder of the performance. I have a vivid recollection of the judge trying to catch one that had lit on his knee, and of its evading him with the pertinacity of a living insect. And, even at this time, Wang, still plying his fan, was taking chickens out of hats, making oranges disappear, pulling endless yards of silk from his sleeve, apparently filling the whole area of the basement with goods, that appeared mysteriously from the ground, from his own sleeves, from nowhere! He swallowed knives to the ruin of his digestion for years to come; he dislocated every limb of his body; he reclined in the air, apparently upon nothing. But his crowning performance, which I have never yet seen repeated, was the most weird, mysterious, and astounding. It is my apology for this long intro-duction, my sole excuse for writing this article, and the genesis of this veracious history.

He cleared the ground of its encumbering articles for a space of about fifteen feet square, and then invited us all to walk forward, and again examine it. We did so gravely. There was nothing but the cemented pavement below to be seen or felt. He then asked for the loan of a handkerchief; and, as I chanced to be nearest him, I offered mine. He took it, and spread it open upon the floor.

Over this he spread a large square of silk, and over this, again, a large shawl nearly covering the space he had cleared. He then took a position at one of the points of this rectangle, and began a monotonous chant, rocking his body to and fro in time with the somewhat lugubrious air.

We sat still and waited. Above the chant we could hear the striking of the city clocks, and the occasional rattle of a cart in the street overhead. The absolute watchfulness and expectation, the dim, mysterious half-light of the cellar, falling in a gruesome way upon the misshapen bulk of a Chinese deity in the background, a faint smell of opium-smoke mingling with spice, and the dreadful uncertainty of what we were really waiting for, sent an uncomfortable thrill down our backs, and made us look at each other with a forced and unnatural smile. This feeling was heightened when Hop Sing slowly rose, and, without a word, pointed with his finger to the centre of the shawl.

There was something beneath the shawl. Surely —and something that was not there before ; at first a mere suggestion in relief, a faint outline, but growing more and more distinct and visible every moment. The chant still continued ; the perspiration began to roll from the singer's face ; gradually the hidden object took upon itself a shape and bulk that raised the shawl in its centre some five or six inches. It was now unmistakably the outline of a small but perfect human figure, with extended

arms and legs. One or two of us turned pale.
There was a feeling of general uneasiness, until the
editor broke the silence by a gibe, that, poor as it
was, was received with spontaneous enthusiasm.
Then the chant suddenly ceased. Wang arose, and
with a quick, dexterous movement, stripped both
shawl and silk away, and discovered, sleeping
peacefully upon my handkerchief, a tiny Chinese
baby.

The applause and uproar which followed this
revelation ought to have satified Wang, even if his
audience was a small one ; it was loud enough to
awaken the baby—a pretty little boy about a year
old, looking like a Cupid cut out of sandal-wood.
He was whisked away almost as mysteriously as he
appeared. When Hop Sing returned my handkerchief to me with a bow, I asked if the juggler was
the father of the baby. "No sabe !" said the imperturbable Hop Sing, taking refuge in that Spanish
form of non-committalism so common in California.

"But does he have a new baby for every performance ?" I asked. "Perhaps : who knows?"
"But what will become of this one ? "   "Whatever
you choose gentlemen," replied Hop Sing with a
courteous inclination. "It was born here ; you are
its godfathers."

There were two characteristic peculiarities of
any Californian assemblage in 1856—it was quick
to take a hint, and generous to the point of prodi-
gality in its response to any charitable appeal.

No matter how sordid or avaricious the individual, he could not resist the infection of sympathy. I doubled the points of my handkerchief into a bag, dropped a coin into it, and, without a word, passed it to the judge. He quietly added a twenty-dollar gold piece, and passed it to the next. When it was returned to me, it contained over a hundred dollars. I knotted the money in the handkerchief, and gave it to Hop Sing.

" For the baby, from its godfathers."

" But what name ? " said the judge. There was a running fire of "Erebus," "Nox," "Plutus," "Terra Cotta," "Antæus," etc. Finally the question was referred to our host.

" Why not keep his own name ? " he said quietly, —" Wan Lee." And he did.

And thus was Wan Lee, on the night of Friday, the 5th of March, 1856, born into this veracious chronicle.

The last form of the *Northern Star* for the 19th of July, 1865, the only daily paper published in Klamath County, had just gone to press; and at 3 a.m. I was putting aside my proofs and manuscripts, preparatory to going home, when I discovered a letter lying under some sheets of paper, which I must have overlooked. The envelope was considerably soiled; it had no post-mark; but I had no difficulty in recognising the hand of my friend Hop Sing. I opened it hurriedly, and read as follows :—

"My DEAR SIR,—I do not know whether the bearer will suit you; but unless the office of 'devil' in your newspaper is a purely technical one, I think he has all the qualities required. He is very quick, active, and intelligent; understands English better than he speaks it; and makes up for any defect by his habits of observation and imitation. You have only to show him how to do a thing once, and he will repeat it, whether it is an offence or a virtue. But you certainly know him already. You are one of his godfathers; for is he not Wan Lee, the reputed son of Wang the conjurer, to whose performances I had the honour to introduce you? But perhaps you have forgotten it.

" I shall send him with a gang of coolies to Stockton, thence by express to your town. If you can use him there, you will do me a favour, and probably save his life, which is at present in great peril from the hands of the younger members of your Christian and highly-civilized race who attend the enlightened schools in San Francisco.

" He has acquired some singular habits and customs from his experience of Wang's profession, which he followed for some years—until he became too large to go in a hat, or be produced from his father's sleeve. The money you left with me has been expended on his education. He has gone through the Tri-literal Classics, but, I think, without much benefit. He knows but little of Confucius, and absolutely nothing of Mencius. Owing to the negligence of his father he associated, perhaps, too much with American children.

" I should have answered your letter before by post; but I thought that Wan Lee himself would be a better messenger for the.

"Yours respectfully,

"HOP SING."

And this was the long-delayed answer to my letter to Hop Sing. But where was "the bearer"? How was the letter delivered? I summoned hastily the foreman, printers, and office-boy, but without eliciting anything. No one had seen the letter delivered, nor knew anything of the bearer. A few days later, I had a visit from my laundry-man, Ah Ri.

"You wantee debbil? All lightee : me catchee him."

He returned in a few moments with a bright-looking Chinese boy, about ten years old, with whose appearance and general intelligence I was so greatly impressed that I engaged him on the spot. When the business was concluded, I asked his name.

"Wan Lee," said the boy.

"What! Are you the boy sent out by Hop Sing? What the devil do you mean by not coming here before? and how did you deliver that letter?"

Wan Lee looked at me, and laughed. "Me pitchee in top side window."

I did not understand. He looked for a moment perplexed, and then, snatching the letter out of my hand, ran down the stairs. After a moment's pause, to my great astonishment, the letter came flying in the window, circled twice around the room, and then dropped gently, like a bird, upon the table. Before I had got over my surprise, Wan Lee re-appeared, smiled, looked at the letter and then at me, said, "So, John," and then remained gravely silent. I said nothing further ; but it was understood that this was his first official act.

His next performance, I grieve to say, was not attended with equal success. One of our regular paper-carriers fell sick, and, at a pinch, Wan Lee was ordered to fill his place. To prevent mistakes, he was shown over the route the previous evening, and supplied at about daylight with the usual number of subscribers' copies. He returned, after an hour, in good spirits, and without the papers. He had delivered them all, he said.

Unfortunately for Wan Lee, at about eight o'clock indignant subscribers began to arrive at the office. They had received their copies: but how? In the form of hard-pressed cannon-balls, delivered by a single shot, and a mere *tour de force*, through the glass of bedroom windows. They had received them full in the face, like a base ball, if they happened to be up and stirring ; they had received them in quarter-sheets, tucked in at separate windows ; they had found them in the chimney, pinned against the door, shot through attic-windows, delivered in long slips through convenient keyholes, stuffed into ventilators, and occupying the same can with the morning's milk. One subscriber, who waited for some time at the office-door to have a personal interview with Wan Lee (then comfortably locked in my bedroom), told me, with tears of rage in his eyes, that he had been awakened at five o'clock by a most hideous yelling below his windows ; that, on rising in great agitation, he was startled by the sudden appearance of

the *Northern Star*, rolled hard, and bent into the
form of a boomerang, or East Indian club, that
sailed into the window, described a number of
fiendish circles in the room, knocked over the light,
slapped the baby's face, "took" him (the subscriber) " in the jaw " and then returned out of the
window, and dropped helplessly in the area.
During the rest of the day, wads and strips of
soiled paper, purporting to be copies of the
Northern Star of that morning's issue, were brought
indignantly to the office. An admirable editorial
on " The Resources of Humboldt County," which
I had constructed the evening before, and which, I
had reason to believe, might have changed the
whole balance of trade during the ensuing year,
and left San Francisco bankrupt at her wharves,
was in this way lost to the public.

It was deemed advisable for the next three weeks
to keep Wan Lee closely confined to the printing-
office, and the purely mechanical part of the business. Here he developed a surprising quickness
and adaptability, winning even the favour and good
will of the printers and foreman, who at first looked
upon his introduction into the secrets of their trade
as fraught with the gravest political significance.
He learned to set type readily and neatly, his
wonderful skill in manipulation aiding him in the
mere mechanical act, and his ignorance of the language confining him simply to the mechanical
effort, confirming the printer's axiom, that the

C

printer who considers or follows the ideas of his copy makes a poor compositor. He would set up deliberately long diatribes against himself, composed by his fellow-printers, and hung on his hook as copy, and even such short sentences as " Wan Lee is the devil's own imp." " Wan Lee is a Mongolian rascal," and bring the proof to me with happiness beaming from every tooth, and satisfaction shining in his huckleberry eyes.

It was not long, however, before he learned to retaliate on his mischievous persecutors. I remember one instance in which his reprisal came very near involving me in a serious misunderstanding. Our foreman's name was Webster ; and Wan Lee presently learned to know and recognize the individual and combined letters of his name. It was during a political campaign ; and the eloquent and fiery Col. Starbottle of Siskyou had delivered an effective speech, which was reported especially for the *Northern Star*. In a very sublime peroration, Col. Starbottle had said, " In the language of the godlike Webster, I repeat "—and here followed the quotation, which I have forgotten. Now, it chanced that Wan Lee, looking over the galley after it had been revised, saw the name of his chief persecutor, and, of course, imagined the quotation his. After the form was locked up, Wan Lee took advantage of Webster's absence to remove the quotation, and substitute a thin piece of lead, of the same size as the type, engraved with Chinese characters, making a

sentence, which, I had reason to believe, was an utter
and abject confession of the incapacity and offen-
siveness of the Webster family generally, and exceedingly eulogistic of Wan Lee himself personally.

The next morning's paper contained Colonel
Starbottle's speech in full, in which it appeared
that the "godlike" Webster had, on one occasion,
uttered his thoughts in excellent but perfectly
enigmatical Chinese. The rage of Col. Starbottle
knew no bounds. I have a vivid recollection of
that admirable man walking into my office, and
demanding a retractation of the statement.

"But, my dear sir," I asked, "are you willing to
deny, over your own signature, that Webster ever
uttered such a sentence? Dare you deny, that, with
Mr. Webster's well-known attainments, a knowledge of Chinese might not have been among the
number? Are you willing to submit a translation
suitable to the capacity of our readers, and deny,
upon your honour as a gentleman, that the late
Mr. Webster ever uttered such a sentiment? If
you are, sir, I am willing to publish your denial."

The colonel was not, and left, highly indignant.

Webster, the foreman, took it more coolly.
Happily, he was unaware that, for two days after,
Chinamen from the laundries, from the gulches,
from the kitchens, looked in the front office door,
with faces beaming with sardonic delight; that
three hundred extra copies of the *Star* were
ordered for the wash-houses on the river. He only

knew that, during the day, Wan Lee occasionally went off into convulsive spasms, and that he was obliged to kick him into consciousness again. A week after the occurrence, I called Wan Lee into my office.

"Wan," I said gravely, "I should like you to give me, for my own personal satisfaction, a translation of that Chinese sentence which my gifted countryman, the late godlike Webster, uttered upon a public occasion." Wan Lee looked at me intently, and then the slightest possible twinkle crept into his black eyes. Then he replied with equal gravity—

"Mishtel Webstel, he say, 'China boy makee me belly much foolee. China boy makee me heap sick.'" Which I have reason to think was true.

But I fear I am giving but one side, and not the best, of Wan Lee's character. As he imparted it to me, his had been a hard life. He had known scarcely any childhood : he had no recollection of a father or mother. The conjurer Wang had brought him up. He had spent the first seven years of his life in appearing from baskets, in dropping out of hats, in climbing ladders, in putting his little limbs out of joint in posturing. He had lived in an atmosphere of trickery and deception. He had learned to look upon mankind as dupes of their senses : in fine, if he had thought at all, he would have been a sceptic ; if he had been a little older, he would have been a cynic ; if he had

been older still, he would have been a philosopher.
As it was, he was a little imp. A good-natured
imp it was, too—an imp whose moral nature had
never been awakened—an imp up for a holiday,
and willing to try virtue as a diversion. I don't
know that he had any spiritual nature. He was
very superstitious. He carried about with him a
hideous little porcelain god, which he was in the
habit of alternately reviling and propitiating. He
was too intelligent for the commoner Chinese vices
of stealing or gratuitous lying. Whatever discipline he practised was taught by his intellect.

I am inclined to think that his feelings were not
altogether unimpressible, although it was almost
impossible to extract an expression from him ; and
I conscientiously believe he became attached to
those that were good to him. What he might have
become under more favourable conditions than the
bondsman of an overworked, under-paid literary
man, I don't know : I only know that the scant,
irregular, impulsive kindnesses that I showed him
were gratefully received. He was very loyal and
patient, two qualities rare in the average American
servant. He was like Malvolio, " sad and civil "
with me. Only once, and then under great provocation, do I remember of his exhibiting any impa-
tience. It was my habit, after leaving the office at
night, to take him with me to my rooms, as the
bearer of any supplemental or happy after-thought,
in the editorial way, that might occur to me before

the paper went to press. One night I had been scribbling away past the usual hour of dismissing Wan Lee, and had become quite oblivious of his presence in a chair near my door, when suddenly I became aware of a voice saying in plaintive accents, something that sounded like " Chy Lee."

I faced around sternly.

" What did you say ? "

" Me say, ' Chy Lee.' "

" Well ? " I said impatiently.

" You sabe, ' How do, John ' ? "

" Yes."

" You sabe, 'So long, John ' ? "

" Yes."

"Well, ' Chy Lee ' allee same ! "

I understood him quite plainly. It appeared that " Chy Lee " was a form of " good night," and that Wan Lee was anxious to go home. But an instinct of mischief, which, I fear, I possessed in common with him, impelled me to act as if oblivious of the hint. I muttered something about not understanding him, and again bent over my work. In a few minutes I heard his wooden shoes pattering pathetically over the floor. I looked up. He was standing near the door.

" You no sabe, ' Chy Lee ' ? "

" No," I said sternly.

" You sabe muchee big foolee ! allee same ! "

And, with this audacity upon his lips, he fled. The next morning, however, he was as meek and patient as before, and I did not recall his offence. As a probable peace-offering, he blacked all my boots—a duty never required of him—including a pair of buff deer-skin slippers and an immense pair of horseman's jack-boots, on which he indulged his remorse for two hours.

I have spoken of his honesty as being a quality of his intellect rather than his principle ; but I recall about this time two exceptions to the rule. I was anxious to get some fresh eggs as a change to the heavy diet of a mining-town ; and, knowing that Wan Lee's countrymen were great poultry-raisers, I applied to him. He furnished me with them regularly every morning, but refused to take any pay, saying that the man did not sell them—a remarkable instance of self-abnegation, as eggs were then worth half a dollar apiece. One morning my neighbour Forster dropped in upon me at breakfast, and took occasion to bewail his own ill fortune, as his hens had lately stopped laying, or wandered off in the bush. Wan Lee, who was present during our colloquy, preserved his characteristic sad taciturnity. When my neighbour had gone, he turned to me with a slight chuckle : " Flostel's hens—Wan Lee's hens allee same ! " His other offence was more serious and ambitious. It was a season of great irregularities in the mails, and Wan Lee had heard me deplore the delay in the delivery of my letters and newspapers. On arriving at my office one day, I was amazed to

find my table covered with letters, evidently just
from the post-office, but, unfortunately, not one
addressed to me. I turned to Wan Lee, who
was surveying them with a calm satisfaction, and
demanded an explanation. To my horror he
pointed to an empty mail-bag in the corner, and
said, "Postman he say, 'No lettee, John; no
lettee, John.' Postman plentee lie! Postman no
good. Me catchee lettee last night allee same!"
Luckily it was still early : the mails had not been
distributed. I had a hurried interview with the
postmaster : and Wan Lee's bold attempt at rob-
bing the United States mail was finally condoned
by the purchase of a new mail-bag, and the whole
affair thus kept a secret.

If my liking for my little Pagan page had not
been sufficient, my duty to Hop Sing was enough,
to cause me to take Wan Lee with me when I returned to San Francisco after my two years' experience with the *Northern Star.* I do not think
he contemplated the change with pleasure. I at-
tributed his feelings to a nervous dread of crowded
public streets (when he had to go across town for
me on an errand, he always made a circuit of the
outskirts), to his dislike for the discipline of the
Chinese and English school to which I proposed
to send him, to his fondness for the free, vagrant
life of the mines, to sheer wilfulness. That it
might have been a superstitious premonition did
not occur to me until long after.

Nevertheless, it really seemed as if the opportunity I had long looked for and confidently expected had come—the opportunity of placing Wan
Lee under gently restraining influences, of subject-
ing him to a life and experience that would draw
out of him what good my superficial care and ill-
regulated kindness could not reach. Wan Lee was
placed at the school of a Chinese missionary—an
intelligent and kind-hearted clergyman, who had
shown great interest in the boy, and who, better
than all, had a wonderful faith in him. A home
was found for him in the family of a widow, who
had a bright and interesting daughter about two
years younger than Wan Lee. It was this bright,
cheery, innocent, and artless child that touched and
reached a depth in the boy's nature that hitherto
had been unsuspected; that awakened a moral
susceptibility which had lain for years insensible
alike to the teachings of society, or the ethics of
the theologian.

These few brief months—bright with a promise
that we never saw fulfilled—must have been happy
ones to Wan Lee. He worshipped his little friend
with something of the same superstition, but without any of the caprice, that he bestowed upon his
porcelain Pagan god. It was his delight to walk
behind her to school, carrying her books—a service
always fraught with danger to him from the little
hands of his Caucasian Christian brothers. He
made her the most marvellous toys; he would cut

out of carrots and turnips the most astonishing roses and tulips; he made life-like chickens out of melon-seeds; he constructed fans and kites, and was singularly proficient in the making of dolls' paper dresses. On the other hand, she played and sang to him, taught him a thousand little prettinesses and refinements only known to girls, gave him a yellow ribbon for his pig-tail, as best suiting his complexion, read to him, showed him wherein he was original and valuable, took him to Sunday school with her, against the precedents of the school, and, small-woman-like, triumphed. I wish I could add here, that she effected his conversion, and made him give up his porcelain idol. But I am telling a true story; and this little girl was quite content to fill him with her own Christian goodness, without letting him know that he was changed. So they got along very well together —this little Christian girl, with her shining cross hanging around her plump, white little neck; and this dark little Pagan, with his hideous porcelain god hidden away in his blouse.

There were two days of that eventful year which will long be remembered in San Francisco —two days when a mob of her citizens set upon and killed unarmed, defenceless foreigners because they were foreigners, and of another race, religion, and colour, and worked for what wages they could get. There were some public men so timid that, seeing this, they thought that the end of the world had come. There were some eminent statesmen, whose names I am ashamed to write here, who began to think that the passage in the Constitution which guarantees civil and religious liberty to every citizen or foreigner was a mistake. But there were, also, some men who were not so easily frightened; and in twenty-four hours we had things so arranged that the timid men could wring their hands in safety, and the eminent statesmen utter their doubts without hurting anybody or anything. And in the midst of this I got a note from Hop Sing, asking me to come to him immediately.

I found his warehouse closed, and strongly guarded by the police against any possible attack of the rioters. Hop Sing admitted me through a barred grating with his usual imperturbable calm, but, as it seemed to me, with more than his usual seriousness. Without a word, he took my hand, and led me to the rear of the room, and thence down stairs into the basement. It was dimly lighted; but there was something lying on the floor covered by a shawl. As I approached he drew the shawl away with a sudden gesture, and revealed Wan Lee, the Pagan, lying there dead.

Dead, my reverend friends, dead—stoned to death in the streets of San Francisco, in the year of grace 1869, by a mob of half-grown boys and Christian school-children !

As I put my hand reverently upon his breast, I felt something crumbling beneath his blouse. I looked inquiringly at Hop Sing. He put his hand between the folds of silk, and drew out something with the first bitter smile I had ever seen on the face of that Pagan gentleman.

It was Wan Lee's porcelain god, crushed by a stone from the hands of those Christian iconoclasts!

THE ROSE OF TUOLUMNE.

CHAPTER I.

I T was nearly two o'clock in the morning. The lights were out in Robinson's Hall, where there had been dancing and revelry; and the moon, riding high, painted the black windows with silver. The cavalcade, that an hour ago had shocked the sedate pines with song and laughter, were all dispersed. One enamoured swain had ridden east, another west, another north, another south; and the object of their adoration, left within her bower at Chemisal Ridge, was calmly going to bed.

I regret that I am not able to indicate the exact stage of that process. Two chairs were already filled with delicate inwrappings and white confusion; and the young lady herself, half-hidden in the silky threads of her yellow hair, had at one time borne a faint resemblance to a partly-husked ear of Indian corn. But she was now clothed in that one long, formless garment that makes all women equal; and the round shoulders and neat waist, that an hour ago had been so fatal to the peace of mind of Four Forks, had utterly disappeared. The face above it was very pretty: the foot below, albeit shapely, was not small. " The flowers, as a general thing, don't raise their heads *much* to look after me," she had said with superb frankness to one of her lovers.

The expression of the "Rose" to-night was contentedly placid. She walked slowly to the window, and, making the smallest possible peep-hole through the curtain, looked out. The motionless figure of a horseman still lingered on the road, with an excess of devotion that only a coquette, or a woman very much in love, could tolerate. The "Rose," at that moment, was neither, and, after a reasonable pause, turned away, saying quite audibly that it was "too ridiculous for anything." As she came back to her dressing-table, it was noticeable that she walked steadily and erect, without that slight affectation of lameness common to people with whom bare feet are only an episode. Indeed, it was only four years ago, that without shoes or stockings, a long-limbed, colty girl, in a waistless calico gown, she had leaped from the tailboard of her father's emigrant-wagon when it first drew up at Chemisal Ridge. Certain wild habits of the "Rose" had outlived transplanting and cultivation.

A knock at the door surprised her. In another moment she had leaped into bed, and with darkly-frowning eyes, from its secure recesses demanded "Who's there?"

An apologetic murmur on the other side of the door was the response.

"Why, father !—is that you?"

There were further murmurs, affirmative, deprecatory, and persistent.

"Wait," said the "Rose." She got up, unlocked the door, leaped nimbly into bed again, and said, "Come."

The door opened timidly. The broad, stooping shoulders, and grizzled head, of a man past the middle age, appeared : after a moment's hesitation, a pair of large, diffident feet, shod with canvas slippers, concluded to follow. When the apparition was complete, it closed the door softly, and stood there—a very shy ghost indeed—with apparently more than the usual spiritual indisposition to begin a conversation. The "Rose" resented this impatiently, though, I fear, not altogether intelligibly.

"Do, father, I declare !"

"You was abed, Jinny," said Mr. McClosky slowly, glancing, with a singular mixture of masculine awe and paternal pride, upon the two chairs and their contents—"you was abed and ondressed."

"I was."

"Surely," said Mr. McClosky, seating himself on the extreme edge of the bed, and painfully tucking his feet away under it,—"surely." After a pause, he rubbed a short, thick, stumpy beard, that bore a general resemblance to a badly-worn blackingbrush, with the palm of his hand, and went on, "You had a good time, Jinny?"

"Yes, father."

"They was all there?"

"Yes, Rance and York and Ryder and Jack."

"And Jack!" Mr. McClosky endeavoured to throw an expression of arch inquiry into his small, tremulous eyes; but meeting the unabashed, widely-opened lid of his daughter, he winked rapidly, and blushed to the roots of his hair.

"Yes, Jack was there," said Jenny, without change of colour, orthe least self-consciousness in her great grey eyes; "and he came home with me." She paused a moment, locking her two hands under her head, and assuming a more comfortable position on the pillow. "He asked me that same question again, father, and I said, 'Yes.' It's to be —soon. We're going to live at Four Forks, in his own house; and next winter we're going to Sacramento. I suppose it's all right, father, eh?" She emphasized the question with a slight kick through the bed-clothes, as the parental McClosky had fallen into an abstract reverie.

"Yes, surely," said Mr. McClosky, recovering himself with some confusion. After a pause, he looked down at the bed-clothes, and, patting them tenderly, continued, "You couldn't have done better, Jinny. They isn't a girl in Tuolumne ez could strike it ez rich as you hev—even if they got the chance." He paused again, and then said, "Jinny?"

"Yes, father."

"You'se in bed, and ondressed?"

"Yes."

"You couldn't," said Mr. McClosky, glancing

hopelessly at the two chairs, and slowly rubbing his chin—"you couldn't dress yourself again, could yer?"

"Why, father!"

"Kinder get yourself into them things again?" he added hastily. "Not all of 'em, you know, but some of 'em. Not if I helped you—sorter stood by, and lent a hand now and then with a strap, or a buckle, or a necktie, or a shoestring?" he continued, still looking at the chairs, and evidently trying to boldly familiarize himself with their contents.

",Are you crazy, father?" demanded Jenny, suddenly sitting up, with a portentous switch of her yellow mane. Mr. McClosky rubbed one side of his beard, which already had the appearance of having been quite worn away by that process, and faintly dodged the question.

"Jinny," he said, tenderly stroking the bed-clothes as he spoke, "this yer's what's the matter. Thar is a stranger down stairs—a stranger to you, lovey, but a man ez I've knowed a long time. He's been here about an hour; and he'll be here ontil fower o'clock, when the up-stage passes. Now I wants ye, Jinny dear, to get up and come down stairs, and kinder help me pass the time with him. It's no use, Jinny," he went on, gently raising his hand to deprecate any interruption—"its no use! He won't go to bed; he won't play keerds; whisky don't take no effect on him. Ever since I knowed

D

‹ ··

him, he was the most onsatisfactory critter to hev round——"

"What do you have him round for, then?" interrupted Miss Jenny, sharply.

Mr. McClosky's eyes fell. "Ef he hedn't kem out of his way to-night to do me a good turn, I wouldn't ask ye, Jinny. I wouldn't, so help me! But I thought, ez I couldn't do anything with him, you might come down, and sorter fetch him, Jinny, as you did the others."

Miss Jenny shrugged her pretty shoulders.

"Is he old, or young?"

"He's young enough, Jinny; but he knows a power of things."

"What does he do?"

"Not much, I reckon. He's got money in the mill at Four Forks. He travels round a good deal. I've heard, Jinny, that he's a poet—writes them rhymes, you know." Mr. McClosky here appealed submissively but directly to his daughter. He remembered that she had frequently been in receipt of printed elegaic couplets known as "mottoes," containing enclosures equllay saccharine.

Miss Jenny slightly curled her pretty lip. She had that fine contempt for the illusions of fancy which belongs to the perfectly healthy young animal.

"Not," continued Mr. McClosky, rubbing his head reflectively, "not ez I'd advise ye, Jinny, to say anything to him about poetry. It ain't twenty

minutes ago ez *I* did. I set the whisky afore him
in the parlour. I wound up the music-box, and set
it goin'. Then I sez to him, sociable-like and free,
'Jest consider yourself in your own house, and
repeat what you allow to be your finest produc-
tion,' and he raged. That man, Jinny, jest raged !
Thar's no end of the names he called me. You see,
Jinny," continued Mr. McClosky, apologetically,
" he's known me a long time."

But his daughter had already dismissed the
question with her usual directness. " I'll be down
in a few moments, father," she said, after a pause,
" but don't say anything to him about it—don't say
I was abed."

Mr. McClosky's face beamed. " You was allers
a good girl, Jinny," he said, dropping on one knee
the better to imprint a respectful kiss on her forehead. But Jenny caught him by the wrists, and for
a moment held him captive. " Father," said she,
trying to fix his shy eyes with the clear, steady
glance of her own, "all the girls that were there
to-night had some one with them. Mame Robinson
had her aunt ; Lucy Rance had her mother ; Kate
Pierson had her sister—all, except me, had some
other woman. Father dear," her lip trembled just
a little, " I wish mother hadn't died when I was so
small. I wish there was some other woman in the
family besides me. I ain't lonely with you, father
dear ; but if there was only some one, you know,
when the time comes for John and me——"

Her voice here suddenly gave out, but not her brave eyes, that were still fixed earnestly upon his face. Mr. McClosky, apparently tracing out a pattern on the bedquilt, essayed words of comfort.

"Thar ain't one of them gals, ez you've named, Jinny, ez could do what you've done with a whole Noah's ark of relations at their backs! Thar ain't one ez wouldn't sacrifice her nearest relation to make the strike that you hev. Ez to mothers, maybe, my dear, you're doin' better without one." He rose suddenly, and walked toward the door. When he reached it, he turned, and, in his old deprecating manner, said, "Don't be long, Jinny," smiled, and vanished from the head downward, his canvas slippers asserting themselves resolutely to the last.

When Mr. McClosky reached his parlour again, his troublesome guest was not there. The decanter stood on the table untouched ; three or four books lay upon the floor ; a number of photographic views of the Sierras were scattered over the sofa ; two sofa-pillows, a newspaper, and a Mexican blanket lay on the carpet, as if the late occupant of the room had tried to read in a recumbent position. A French window, opening upon a veranda, which never before in the history of the house had been unfastened, now betrayed by its waving lace curtain the way that the fugitive had escaped. Mr. McClosky heaved a sigh of despair. He looked at the gorgeous carpet, purchased in Sacramento at a fabulous price, at the crimson satin and rosewood furniture, unparalleled in the history of Tuolumne, at the massively-framed pictures on the walls, and looked beyond it, through the open window, to the reckless man, who, fleeing these sybaritic allurements, was smoking a cigar upon the moonlit road. This room, which had so often awed the youth of Tuolumne into filial respect, was evidently a failure. It remained to be seen if the "Rose" herself had lost her fragrance. "I reckon Jinny will fetch him yet," said Mr. McClosky with parental faith.

He stepped from the window upon the veranda ; but he had scarcely done this, before his figure was detected by the stranger, who at once crossed the road. When within a few feet of McClosky, he stopped. "You persistent old plantigrade!" he said in a low voice, audible only to the person addressed, and a face full of affected anxiety, "why don't you go to bed ? Didn't I tell you to go and leave me here alone ? In the name of all that's idiotic and imbecile, why do you continue to shuffle about here ? Or are you trying to drive me crazy with your presence, as you have with that wretched music-box that I've just dropped under yonder tree ? It's an hour and a half yet before the stage passes ; do you think, do you imagine for a single moment, that I can tolerate you until then, eh ? Why don't you speak ? Are you asleep ? You don't mean to say that you have the audacity to add somnambulism to your other weaknesses? You're not low enough to repeat yourself under any such weak pretext as that, eh?"

A fit of nervous coughing ended this extraordinary exordium; and half sitting, half leaning against the veranda, Mr. McClosky's guest turned his face, and part of a slight elegant figure, toward his host. The lower portion of this upturned face wore an habitual expression of fastidious discontent, with an occasional line of physical suffering. But the brow above was frank and critical; and a pair of dark, mirthful eyes sat in playful judgment over the super-sensitive mouth and its suggestion.

"I allowed to go to bed, Ridgeway," said Mr. McClosky, meekly; "but my girl Jinny's jist got back from a little tear-up at Robinson's, and ain't inclined to turn in yet. You know what girls is. So I thought we three would jist have a social chat together to pass away the time."

"You mendacious old hypocrite! She got back an hour ago," said Ridgeway, "as that savage-looking escort of hers, who has been haunting the house ever since, can testify. My belief is, that, like an enterprising idiot as you are, you've dragged that girl out of her bed, that we might mutually bore each other."

Mr. McClosky was too much stunned by this evidence of Ridgeway's apparently superhuman penetration to reply. After enjoying his host's

confusion for a moment with his eyes, Ridgeway's
mouth asked grimly—

" And who is this girl, any way ? "

" Nancy's."

" Your wife's ? "

" Yes. But look yar, Ridgeway," said McClosky,
laying one hand imploringly on Ridgeway's sleeve,
"not a word about her to Jinny. She thinks her
mother's dead—died in Missouri. Eh ! "

Ridgeway nearly rolled from the veranda in an
excess of rage. "Good God! Do you mean to
say that you have been concealing from her a fact
that any day, any moment, may come to her ears ?
That you've been letting her grow up in ignorance
of something that by this time she might have
outgrown and forgotten ? That you have been, like
a besotted old ass, all these years slowly forging
a thunderbolt that anyone may crush her with ?
That—" but here Ridgeway's cough took possession
of his voice, and even put a moisture into his dark
eyes, as he looked at McClosky's aimless hand
feebly employed upon his beard.

" But," said McClosky, " look how she's done !
She's held her head as high as any of 'em. She's
to be married in a month to the richest man in the
county ; and," he added cunningly, " Jack Ashe
ain't the kind o' man to sit by and hear anything
said of his wife or her relations, you bet ! But
hush—that's her foot on the stairs. She's cum-
min'. "

She came. I don't think the French window ever held a finer view than when she put aside the curtains and stepped out. She had dressed herself simply and hurriedly, but with a woman's knowledge of her best points ; so that you got the long curves of her shapely limbs, the shorter curves of her round waist and shoulders, the long sweep of her yellow braids, the light of her grey eyes, and even the delicate rose of her complexion, without knowing how it was delivered to you.

The introduction by Mr. McClosky was brief. When Ridgeway had got over the fact that it was two o'clock in the morning, and that the cheek of this Tuolumne goddess nearest him was as dewy and fresh as an infant's, that she looked like Marguerite, without, probably, ever having heard of Goethe's heroine, he talked, I dare say, very sensibly. When Miss Jenny—who from her childhood had been brought up among the sons of Anak, and who was accustomed to have the supremacy of our noble sex presented to her as a physical fact— found herself in the presence of a new and strange power in the slight and elegant figure beside her, she was at first frightened and cold. But finding that this power, against which the weapons of her own physical charms were of no avail, was a kindly one, albeit general, she fell to worshipping it, after the fashion of woman, and casting before it the fetishes and other idols of her youth. She even confessed to it. So that, in half an hour, Ridgeway was in possession of all the facts connected with her life, and a great many, I fear, of her fancies—except one. When Mr. McClosky found the young people thus amicably disposed, he calmly went to sleep.

It was a pleasant time to each. To Miss Jenny it had the charm of novelty ; and she abandoned herself to it, for that reason, much more freely and innocently than her companion, who knew something more of the inevitable logic of the position. I do not think, however, he had any intention of love-making. I do not think he was at all conscious of being in the attitude. I am quite positive he would have shrunk from the suggestion of disloyalty to the one woman whom he admitted to himself he loved. But, like most poets, he was much more true to an idea than a fact, and having a very lofty conception of womanhood, with a very sanguine nature, he saw in each new face the possibilities of a realization of his ideal. It was, perhaps, an unfortunate thing for the women, particularly as he brought to each trial a surprising freshness, which was very deceptive, and quite distinct from the *blasé* familiarity of the man of gallantry. It was this perennial virginity of the affections that most endeared him to the best women, who were prone to exercise toward him a chivalrous protection—as of one likely to go astray, unless looked after—and indulged in the dangerous combination of sentiment with the highest maternal instincts.

It was this quality which caused Jenny to recognize in him a certain boyishness that required her womanly care, and even induced her to offer to accompany him to the cross-roads when the time' for his departure arrived. With her superior knowledge of woodcraft and the locality, she would have kept him from being lost. I wot not but that she would have protected him from bears or wolves, but chiefly, I think, from the feline fascinations of Mame Robinson and Lucy Rance, who might be lying in wait for this tender young poet. Nor did she cease to be thankful that Providence had, so to speak, delivered him as a trust into her hands.

It was a lovely night. The moon swung low, and languished softly on the snowy ridge beyond. There were quaint odours in the still air; and a strange incense from the woods perfumed their young blood, and seemed to swoon in their pulses. Small wonder that they lingered on the white road, that their feet climbed, unwillingly, the little hill where they were to part, and that, when they at last reached it, even the saving grace of speech seemed to have forsaken them.

For there they stood alone. There was no sound nor motion in earth, or woods, or heaven. They might have been the one man and woman for whom this goodly earth that lay at their feet, rimmed with the deepest azure, was created. And, seeing this, they turned toward each other with a sudden instinct, and their hands met, and then their lips in one long kiss.

And then out of the mysterious distance came the sound of voices, and the sharp clatter of hoofs and wheels, and Jenny slid away—a white moonbeam—from the hill. For a moment she glimmered through the trees, and then, reaching the house, passed her sleeping father on the veranda, and, darting into her bedroom, locked the door, threw open the window, and, falling on her knees beside it, leaned her hot cheeks upon her hands, and listened. In a few moments she was rewarded by the sharp clatter of hoofs on the stony road ; but it was only a horseman, whose dark figure was swiftly lost in the shadows of the lower road. At another time she might have recognized the man ; but her eyes and ears were now all intent on something else. It came presently, with dancing lights, a musical rattle of harness, a cadence of hoofbeats, that set her heart to beating in unison— and was gone. A sudden sense of loneliness came over her ; and tears gathered in her sweet eyes.

She arose, and looked around her. There was the little bed, the dressing-table, the roses that she had worn last night, still fresh and blooming in the little vase. Everything was there ; but everything looked strange. The roses should have been withered, for the party seemed so long ago. She could hardly remember when she had worn this dress that lay upon the chair. So she came back to the window, and sank down beside it, with her cheek a trifle paler, leaning on her hand, and her long braids reaching to the floor. The stars paled slowly, like her cheek; yet, with eyes that saw not, she still looked from the window for the coming dawn.

It came, with violet deepening into purple, with purple flushing into rose, with rose shining into silver, and glowing into gold. The straggling line of the black picket-fence below, that had faded away with the stars, came back with the sun. What was that object moving by the fence? Jenny raised her head, and looked intently. It was a man endeavouring to climb the pickets, and falling backward with each attempt. Suddenly she started to her feet, as if the rosy flushes of the dawn had crimsoned her from forehead to shoulders; then she stood, white as the wall, with her hands clasped upon her bosom; then, with a single bound, she reached the door, and, with flying braids and fluttering skirt, sprang down the stairs, and out to the garden walk. When within a few feet of the fence, she uttered a cry, the first she had given— the cry of a mother over her stricken babe, of a tigress over her mangled cub; and in another moment she had leaped the fence, and knelt beside Ridgeway, with his fainting head upon her breast.

"My boy, my poor, poor boy! who has done this?"

Who, indeed? His clothes were covered with dust; his waistcoat was torn open; and his handkerchief, wet with the blood it could not stanch, fell from a cruel stab beneath his shoulder.

"Ridgeway, my poor boy! tell me what has happened."

Ridgeway slowly opened his heavy blue-veined lids, and gazed upon her. Presently a gleam of mischief came into his dark eyes, a smile stole over his lips as he whispered slowly—

"It—was—your kiss—did it, Jenny dear! I had forgotten how high-priced the article was here. Never mind, Jenny!"—he feebly raised her hand to his white lips—"it was—worth it," and fainted away.

Jenny started to her feet, and looked wildly around her. Then, with a sudden resolution, she stooped over the insensible man, and with one strong effort lifted him in her arms as if he had been a child. When her father, a moment later, rubbed his eyes, and awoke from his sleep upon the veranda, it was to see a goddess, erect and triumphant, striding toward the house with the helpless body of a man lying across that breast where man had never laid before—a goddess at whose imperious mandate he arose, and cast open the doors before her. And then, when she had laid her unconscious burden on the sofa, the goddess fled; and a woman, helpless and trembling, stood before him—a woman that cried out that she

had "killed him," that she was wicked, wicked!"
and that, even saying so, staggered, and fell beside
her late burden. And all that Mr. McClosky could
do was to feebly rub his beard, and say to himself,
vaguely and incoherently, that "Jinny had fetched
him."

CHAPTER II.

BEFORE noon the next day, it was generally
believed throughout Four Forks that Ridgeway
Dent had been attacked and wounded at Chemisal
Ridge by a highwayman, who fled on the approach
of the Wingdam coach. It is to be presumed that
this statement met with Ridgeway's approval, as he
did not contradict it, nor supplement it with any
details. His wound was severe, but not dangerous.
After the first excitement had subsided, there was,
I think, a prevailing impression common to the pro-
vincial mind that his misfortune was the result of
the defective moral quality of his being a stranger,
and was, in a vague sort of a way, a warning to
others, and a lesson to him. "Did you hear how
that San Francisco feller was took down the other
night?" was the average tone of introductory remark. Indeed, there was a general suggestion that
Ridgeway's presence was one that no self-respecting,
high-minded highwayman, honourably conservative
of the best interests of Tuolumne County, could for
a moment tolerate.

Except for the few words spoken on that eventful

morning, Ridgeway was reticent of the past. When Jenny strove to gather some details of the affray that might offer a clue to his unknown assailant, a subtle twinkle in his brown eyes was the only response. When Mr. McClosky attempted the same process, the young gentleman threw abusive epithets, and, eventually slippers, teaspoons, and other lighter articles within the reach of an invalid, at the head of his questioner. "I think he's coming round Jinny," said Mr. McClosky: "he laid for me this morning with a candlestick."

It was about this time that Miss Jenny, having sworn her father to secrecy regarding the manner in which Ridgeway had been carried into the house, conceived the idea of addressing the young man as "Mr. Dent," and of apologising for intruding whenever she entered the room in the discharge of her household duties. It was about this time that she became more rigidly conscientious to those duties, and less general in her attentions. It was at this time that the quality of the invalid's diet improved, and that she consulted him less frequently about it. It was about this time that she began to see more company, that the house was greatly frequented by her former admirers, with whom she rode, walked, and danced. It was about this time also, and when Ridgeway was able to be brought out on the veranda in a chair, that, with great archness of manner, she introduced to him Miss Lucy Ashe, the sister of her betrothed, a flashing brunette, and terrible

heart-breaker of Four Forks. And, in the midst of
this gaiety, she concluded that she would spend a
week with the Robinsons, to whom she owed a visit.
She enjoyed herself greatly there, so much, indeed,
that she became quite hollow-eyed, the result, as
she explained to her father, of a too frequent in-
dulgence in festivity. "You see, father, I won't
have many chances after John and I are married:
you know how queer he is, and I must make the
most of my time;" and she laughed an odd little
laugh, which had lately become habitual to her.
"And how is Mr. Dent getting on?" Her father
replied that he was getting on very well indeed—
so well, in fact, that he was able to leave for San
Francisco two days ago. "He wanted to be remembered to you, Jinny—'remembered kindly'—
yes, they is the very words he used," said Mr.
McClosky, looking down, and consulting one of his
large shoes for corroboration. Miss Jenny was glad
to hear that he was so much better. Miss Jenny
could not imagine anything that pleased her more
than to know that he was so strong as to be able
to rejoin his friends again, who must love him so
much, and be so anxious about him. Her father
thought she would be pleased, and, now that he was
gone, there was really no necessity for her to hurry
back. Miss Jenny, in a high metallic voice, did not
know that she had expressed any desire to stay,
still, if her presence had become distasteful at
home, if her own father was desirous of getting rid

of her, if, when she was so soon to leave his roof for ever, he still begrudged her those few days remaining, if—" "My God, Jinny, so help me!" said Mr. McClosky, clutching despairingly at his beard, "I didn't go for to say anything of the kind. I thought that you—" "Never mind, father," interrupted Jenny, magnanimously, "you misunderstood me: of course you did, you couldn't help it—you're a MAN!" Mr. McClosky, sorely crushed, would have vaguely protested; but his daughter, having relieved herself, after the manner of her sex, with a mental personal application of an abstract statement, forgave him with a kiss.

Nevertheless, for two or three days after her return, Mr. McClosky followed his daughter about the house with yearning eyes, and occasionally with timid, diffident feet. Sometimes he came upon her suddenly at her household tasks, with an excuse so palpably false, and a careless manner so outrageously studied, that she was fain to be embarrassed for him. Later, he took to rambling about the house at night, and was often seen noiselessly passing and repassing through the hall after she had retired. On one occasion, he was surprised, first by sleep, and then by the early-rising Jenny, as he lay on the rug outside her chamber-door. "You treat me like a child, father," said Jenny. "I thought, Jinny," said the father, apologetically— "I thought I heard sounds as if you was takin' on inside, and listenin', I fell asleep." "You dear old

E

simple-minded baby!" said Jenny, looking past her father's eyes, and lifting his grizzled locks one by one with meditative fingers : "what should I be takin' on for? Look how much taller I am than you!" she said, suddenly lifting herself up to the extreme of her superb figure. Then rubbing his head rapidly with both hands, as if she were anointing his hair with some rare unguent, she patted him on the back, and returned to her room. The result of this and one or two other equally sympathetic interviews was to produce a change in Mr. McClosky's manner, which was, if possible, still more discomposing. He grew unjustifiably hilarious, cracked jokes with the servants, and repeated to Jenny humorous stories, with the attitude of facetiousness carefully preserved throughout the entire narration, and the point utterly ignored and forgotten. Certain incidents reminded him of funny things, which invariably turned out to have not the slightest relevancy or application. He occasionally brought home with him practical humorists, with a sanguine hope of setting them going, like the music-box, for his daughter's edification. He essayed the singing of melodies with great freedom of style, and singular limitation of note. He sang "Come haste to the Wedding, Ye Lasses and Maidens," of which he knew a single line, and that incorrectly, as being peculiarly apt and appropriate. Yet away from the house and his daughter's presence, he was silent and distraught. His absence of

mind was particularly noted by his workmen at the
Empire Quartz Mill. "Ef the old man don't look
out and wake up," said his foreman, "he'll hev
them feet of his get under the stamps. When he
ain't givin' his mind to' em, they is altogether too
promiskuss."

A few nights later, Miss Jenny recognized her
father's hand in a timid tap at the door. She
opened it, and he stood before her, with a valise in
his hand, equipped as for a journey. "I takes the
stage to-night, Jinny dear, from Four Forks to
'Frisco. Maybe I may drop in on Jack afore I go.
I'll be back in a week. Good-bye."

"Good-bye." He still held her hand. Presently
he drew her back into the room, closing the door
carefully, and glancing around. There was a look
of profound cunning in his eye as he said slowly—

"Bear up, and keep dark, Jinny dear, and trust
to the old man. Various men has various ways.
Thar is ways as is common, and ways as is un-
common ; ways as is easy, and ways as is oneasy.
Bear up, and keep dark." With this Delphic utterance he put his finger to his lips, and vanished.

It was ten o'clock when he reached Four Forks.
A few minutes later, he stood on the threshold of
that dwelling described by the Four Forks *Sentinel*
as "the palatial residence of John Ashe," and
known to the local satirist as the "ash-box."
"Hevin' to lay by two hours, John," he said to his
prospective son-in-law, as he took his hand at the

door, " a few words of social converse, not on business, but strictly private, seems to be about as
nat'ral a thing as a man can do." This introduction, evidently the result of some study, and plainly
committed to memory, seemed so satisfactory to
Mr. McClosky that he repeated it again, after John
Ashe had led him into his private office, where,
depositing his valise in the middle of the floor, and
sitting down before it, he began carefully to avoid
the eye of his host.   John Ashe, a tall, dark, handsome Kentuckian, with whom even the trifles of
life were evidently full of serious import, waited
with a kind of chivalrous respect the further speech
of his guest.   Being utterly devoid of any sense of
the ridiculous, he always accepted Mr. McClosky
as a grave fact, singular only from his own want of
experience of the class.

"Ores is running light now," said Mr. McClosky
with easy indifference.

John Ashe returned that he had noticed the
same fact in the receipts of the mill at Four
Forks.

Mr. McClosky rubbed his beard, and looked at
his valise, as if for sympathy and suggestion.

"You don't reckon on having any trouble with
any of them chaps as you cut out with Jinny?"

John Ashe, rather haughtily, had never thought
of that.   "I saw Rance hanging round your house
the other night, when I took your daughter home;
but he gave me a wide berth," he added carelessly.

"Surely," said Mr. McClosky, with a peculiar winking of the eye. After a pause, he took a fresh departure from his valise.

"A few words, John, ez between man and man, ez between my daughter's father and her husband who expects to be, is about the thing, I take it, as is fair and square. I kem here to say them. They're about Jinny, my gal."

Ashe's grave face brightened, to Mr. McClosky's evident discomposure.

"Maybe I should have said about her mother; but, the same bein' a stranger to you, I says naterally, ' Jinny.'"

Ashe nodded courteously. Mr. McClosky, with his eyes on his valise, went on.

"It is sixteen year ago as I married Mrs. McClosky in the State of Missouri. She let on, at the time, to be a widder—a widder with one child. When I say let on, I mean to imply that I subsekently found out that she was not a widder, nor a wife; and the father of the child was, so to speak, onbeknowst. Thet child was Jinny—my gal."

With his eyes on his valise, and quietly ignoring the wholly-crimsoned face and swiftly-darkening brow of his host, he continued—

"Many little things sorter tended to make our home in Missouri onpleasant. A disposition to smash furniture, and heave knives around; an incli-nation to howl when drunk, and that frequent; a habitooal use of vulgar language, and a tendency to cuss the casooal visitor—seemed to pint," added Mr. McClosky with submissive hesitation, "that—she—was—so to speak—quite onsuited to the marriage relation in its holiest aspeck."

"Damnation! Why didn't—" burst out John Ashe, erect and furious.

"At the end of two year," continued Mr. McClosky, still intent on the valise, "I allowed I'd get a diworce. Et about thet time, however, Providence sends a circus into thet town, and a feller ez rodé three horses to onct. Hevin' allez a taste for athletic sports, she left town with this feller, leavin' me and Jinny behind. I sent word to her thet, if she would give Jinny to me, we'd call it quits. And she did."

"Tell me," gasped Ashe, "did you ask your daughter to keep this from me; or did she do it of her own accord?"

"She doesn't know it," said Mr. McClosky. "She thinks I'm her father, and that her mother's dead."

"Then, sir, this is your——"

"I don't know," said Mr. McClosky, slowly, "ez I've asked anyone to marry my Jinny. I don't know ez I've persood that ez a biziness, or even taken it up as a healthful recreation."

John Ashe paced the room furiously. Mr. McClosky's eyes left the valise, and followed him curiously. "Where is this woman?" demanded

Ashe, suddenly. McClosky's eyes sought the valise
again.

"She went to Kansas; from Kansas she went
into Texas; from Texas she eventooally came to
Californy. Being here, I've purvided her with
money, when her business was slack, through a
friend."

John Ashe groaned. "She's gettin' rather old
and shaky for hosses, and now does the tight-rope
business and flying trapeze. Never hevin' seen her
perform," continued Mr. McClosky, with conscientious caution, "I can't say how she gets on. On
the bills she looks well. Thar is a poster," said Mr.
McClosky, glancing at Ashe, and opening his valise
—"thar is a poster givin' her performance at
Marysville next month." Mr. McClosky slowly
unfolded a large yellow-and-blue printed poster,
profusely illustrated. "She calls herself 'Mam-
s'elle J. Miglawski, the great Russian Trape-
ziste.'"

John Ashe tore it from his hand. "Of course,"
he said, suddenly facing Mr. McClosky, "you don't
expect me to go on with this?"

Mr. McClosky took up the poster, carefully re-
folded it, and returned it to his valise. "When you
break off with Jinny," he said, quietly, "I don't want
anything said 'bout this. She doesn't know it. She's
a woman, and I reckon you're a white man."

"But what am I to say? How am I to go back
of my word?"

"Write her a note. Say something hez come to your knowledge (don't say what) that makes you break it off. You needn't be afeard Jinny'll ever ask you what."

John Ashe hesitated. He felt he had been cruelly wronged. No gentleman, no Ashe, could go on further in this affair. It was preposterous to think of it. But somehow he felt at the moment very unlike a gentleman, or an Ashe, and was quite sure he should break down under Jenny's steady eyes. But then—he could write to her.

"So ores is about as light here as on the Ridge. Well, I reckon they'll come up before the rains. Good night." Mr. McClosky [took the hand that his host mechanically extended, shook it gravely, and was gone.

When Mr. McClosky, a week later, stepped again upon his own veranda, he saw through the French window the figure of a man in his parlour. Under his hospitable roof, the sight was not unusual ; but, for an instant, a subtle sense of disappointment thrilled him. When he saw it was not the face of Ashe turned towards him, he was relieved ; but when he saw the tawny beard, and quick, passionate eyes of Henry Rance, he felt a new sense of apprehension, so that he fell to rubbing his beard almost upon his very threshold.

Jenny ran into the hall, and seized her father with a little cry of joy. "Father," said Jenny, in

a hurried whisper, "don't mind *him*," indicating
Rance with a toss of her yellow braids : " he's
going soon. And I·think, father, I've done him
wrong. But it's all over with John and me now.
Read that note, and see how he's insulted me."
Her lip quivered ; but she went on, " It's Ridgeway
that he means, father; and I believe it was *his* hand
struck Ridgeway down, or that he knows who did.
But hush, now ! not a word."

She gave him a feverish kiss, and glided back
into the parlour, leaving Mr. McClosky, perplexed
and irresolute, with the note in his hand. He
glanced at it hurriedly, and saw that it was couched
in almost the very words he had suggested. But a
sudden, apprehensive recollection came over him.
He listened ; and, with an exclamation of dismay,
he seized his hat, and ran out of the house, but too
late. At the same moment a quick, nervous footstep was heard upon the veranda ; the French
window flew open, and, with a light laugh of greeting, Ridgeway stepped into the room.

Jenny's finer ear first caught the step. Jenny's
swifter feelings had sounded the depths of hope, of
joy, of despair, before he entered the room. Jenny's
pale face was the only one that met his, self-
possessed and self-reliant, when he stood before
them. An angry flush suffused even the pink
roots of Rance's beard as he rose to his feet. An
ominous fire sprang into Ridgeway's eyes, and a
spasm of hate and scorn passed over the lower part

of his face, and left the mouth and jaw immobile and rigid.

Yet he was the first to speak. "I owe you an apology," he said to Jenny, with a suave scorn that brought the indignant blood back to her cheek, "for this intrusion; but I ask no pardon for withdrawing from the only spot where that man dare confront me with safety."

With an exclamation of rage, Rance sprang toward him. But as quickly Jenny stood between them, erect and menacing. "There must be no quarrel here," she said to Rance. "While I protect your right as my guest, don't oblige me to remind you of mine as your hostess." She turned with a half-deprecatory air to Ridgeway; but he was gone. So was her father. Only Rance remained with a look of ill-concealed triumph on his face.

Without looking at him, she passed toward the door. When she reached it, she turned. "You asked me a question an hour ago. Come to me in the garden, at nine o'clock to-night, and I will answer you. But promise me, first, to keep away from Mr. Dent. Give me your word not to seek him—to avoid him, if he seeks you. Do you promise? It is well."

He would have taken her hand, but she waved him away. In another moment he heard the swift rustle of her dress in the hall, the sound of her feet upon the stair, the sharp closing of her bedroom door, and all was quiet.

And even thus quietly the day wore away; and the night rose slowly from the valley, and overshadowed the mountains with purple wings that fanned the still air into a breeze, until the moon followed it, and lulled everything to rest as with the laying-on of white and benedictory hands. It was a lovely night ; but Henry Rance, waiting impatiently beneath a sycamore at the foot of the garden, saw no beauty in earth or air or sky. A thousand suspicions common to a jealous nature, a vague superstition of the spot, filled his mind with distrust and doubt. "If this should be a trick to keep my hands off that insolent pup!" he muttered. But, even as the thought passed his tongue, a white figure slid from the shrubbery near the house, glided along the line of picket-fence, and then stopped midway, motionless in the moonlight.

It was she. But he scarcely recognized her in the white drapery that covered her head and shoulders and breast. He approached her with a hurried whisper. "Let us withdraw from the moonlight. Everybody can see us here."

"We have nothing to say that cannot be said in the moonlight, Henry Rance," she replied, coldly receding from his proffered hand. She trembled for a moment, as if with a chill, and then suddenly turned upon him. "Hold up your head, and let me look at you! I've known only what men are : let me see what a traitor looks like!"

He recoiled more from her wild face than her

words.   He saw from the first that her hollow
cheeks and hollow eyes were blazing with fever.
He was no coward, but he would have fled.

"You are ill, Jenny," he said; "you had best
return to the house.   Another time——"

"Stop!" she cried hoarsely.   "Move from this
spot, and I'll call for help!   Attempt to leave me
now, and I'll proclaim you the assassin that you
are!"

"It was a fair fight," he said, doggedly.

"Was it a fair fight to creep behind an unarmed
and unsuspecting man?   Was it a fair fight to
try to throw suspicion on some one else?   Was it
a fair fight to deceive me?   Liar and coward that
you are!"

He made a stealthy step toward her with evil
eyes, and a wickeder hand that crept within his
breast.   She saw the motion; but it only stung her
to newer fury.

"Strike!" she said, with blazing eyes, throwing
her hands open before him.   "Strike!   Are you
afraid of the woman who dares you?   Or do you
keep your knife for the backs of unsuspecting men?
Strike, I tell you!   No?   Look, then!"   With a
sudden movement, she tore from her head and
shoulders the thick lace shawl that had concealed
her figure, and stood before him.   "Look!" she
cried, passionately, pointing to the bosom and
shoulders of her white dress, darkly streaked with
faded stains and ominous discoloration—"look!

This is the dress I wore that morning when I found
him lying here—*here*—bleeding from your cowardly
knife. Look! Do you see? This is his blood—
my darling boy's blood!—one drop of which, dead
and faded as it is, is more precious to me than the
whole living pulse of any other man. Look! I
come to you to-night, christened with his blood,
and dare you to strike—dare you to strike him
again through me, and mingle my blood with his.
Strike, I implore you! Strike! if you have any
pity on me, for God's sake! Strike! if you are a
man! Look! Here lay his head on my shoulder;
here I held him to my breast, where never—so help
me my God!—another man—Ah!——"

She reeled against the fence, and something that
had flashed in Rance's hand dropped at her feet;
for another flash and report rolled him over in the
dust: and across his writhing body two men strode,
and caught her ere she fell.

"She has only fainted," said Mr. McClosky.
"Jinny dear, my girl, speak to me!"

"What is this on her dress?" said Ridgeway,
kneeling beside her, and lifting his set and colourless face. At the sound of his voice, the colour
came faintly back to her cheek: she opened her
eyes and smiled.

"It's only your blood, dear boy," she said;
"but look a little deeper, and you'll find my own."

She put up her two yearning hands, and drew
his face and lips down to her own. When Ridge-

way raised his head again, her eyes were closed;
but her mouth still smiled as with the memory of
a kiss.

They bore her to the house, still breathing, but
unconscious. That night the road was filled with
clattering horsemen; and the summoned skill of
the countryside for leagues away gathered at her
couch. The wound, they said, was not essentially
dangerous; but they had grave fears of the shock
to a system that already seemed suffering from
some strange and unaccountable nervous exhaus-
tion. The best medical skill of Tuolumne happened to be young and observing, and waited
patiently an opportunity to account for it. He was
presently rewarded.

For toward morning she rallied, and looked feebly
around. Then she beckoned her father toward her,
and whispered, " Where is he ? "

" They took him away, Jinny dear, in a cart. He
wont trouble you agin." He stopped; for Miss
Jenny had raised herself on her elbow, and was
levelling her black brows at him. But two kicks
from the young surgeon, and a significant motion
towards the door, sent Mr. McClosky away muttering. " How should I know that '*he*' meant
Ridgeway ?" he said, apologetically, as he went and
returned with the young gentleman. The surgeon,
who was still holding her pulse, smiled, and thought
that—with a little care—and attention—the stimu-
lants—might be—diminished—and—he—might

leave—the patient for some hours with perfect safety. He would give further directions to Mr. McClosky—down stairs.

It was with great archness of manner that, half an hour later, Mr. McClosky entered the room with a preparatory cough ; and it was with some disappointment that he found Ridgeway standing quietly by the window, and his daughter apparently fallen into a light doze. He was still more concerned when, after Ridgeway had retired, noticing a pleasant smile playing about her lips, he said softly,

"You was thinking of some one, Jinny ? "

"Yes, father," the grey eyes met his steadily— "of poor John Ashe !"

Her recovery was swift. Nature, that had seemed to stand jealously aloof from her in her mental anguish, was kind to the physical hurt of her favourite child. The superb physique, which had been her charm and her trial, now stood her in good stead. The healing balsam of the pine, the balm of resinous gums, and the rare medicaments of Sierran altitudes touched her as it might have touched the wounded doe ; so that in two weeks she was able to walk about. And when, at the end of the month, Ridgeway returned from a flying visit to San Francisco, and jumped from the Wing- dam coach at four o'clock in the morning, the Rose of Tuolumne, with the dewy petals of either cheek fresh as when first unfolded to his kiss, confronted him on the road.

With a common instinct, their young feet both climbed the little hill now sacred to their thought. When they reached its summit, they were both, I think, a little disappointed. There is a fragrance in the unfolding of a passion that escapes the perfect flower. Jenny thought the night was not as beautiful ; Ridgeway, that the long ride had blunted his perceptions. But they had the frankness to confess it to each other, with the rare delight of such a confession, and the comparison of details which they thought each had forgotten. And with this, and an occasional pitying reference to the blank period when they had not known each other, hand in hand they reached the house.

Mr. McClosky was awaiting them impatiently upon the veranda. When Miss Jenny had slipped upstairs to replace a collar that stood somewhat suspiciously awry, Mr. McClosky drew Ridgeway solemnly aside. He held a large theatre poster in one hand, and an open newspaper in the other.

" I allus said," he remarked, slowly, with the air of merely renewing a suspended conversation—" I allus said that riding three horses to onct wasn't exactly in her line. It would seem that it ain't. From remarks in this yer paper, it would appear that she tried it on at Marysville last week, and broke her neck."

A PASSAGE IN THE LIFE OF MR. JOHN OAKHURST.

H E always thought it must have been fate. Certainly nothing could have been more inconsistent with his habits than to have been in the Plaza at seven o'clock of that midsummer morning. The sight of his colourless face in Sacramento was rare at that season, and, indeed, at any season, anywhere publicly, before two o'clock in the afternoon. Looking back upon it in after-years in the light of a chanceful life, he determined, with the characteristic philosophy of his profession, that it must have been fate.

Yet it is my duty, as a strict chronicler of facts, to state that Mr. Oakhurst's presence there that morning was due to a very simple cause. At exactly half-past six, the bank being then a winner to the amount of twenty thousand dollars, he had risen from the faro-table, relinquished his seat to an accomplished assistant, and withdrawn quietly, without attracting a glance from the silent, anxious faces bowed over the table. But when he entered his luxurious sleeping-room, across the passage-way he was a little shocked at finding the sun streaming through an inadvertently opened window. Some-

F

thing in the rare beauty of the morning, perhaps something in the novelty of the idea, struck him as he was about to close the blinds ; and he hesitated. Then, taking his hat from the table, he stepped down a private staircase into the street.

The people who were abroad at that early hour were of a class quite unknown to Mr. Oakhurst. There were milkmen and hucksters delivering their wares, small tradespeople opening their shops, housemaids sweeping doorsteps, and occasionally a child. These Mr. Oakhurst regarded with a certain cold curiosity, perhaps quite free from the cynical disfavour with which he generally looked upon the more pretentious of his race whom he was in the habit of meeting. Indeed, I think he was not altogether displeased with the admiring glances which these humble women threw after his handsome face and figure, conspicuous even in a country of fine-looking men. While it is very probable that this wicked vagabond, in the pride of his social isolation, would have been coldly indifferent to the advances of a fine lady, a little girl who ran admiringly by his side in a ragged dress had the power to call a faint flush into his colourless cheek. He dismissed her at last, but not until she had found out—what, sooner or later, her large-hearted and discriminating sex inevitably did—that he was exceedingly free and open-handed with his money, and also—what, perhaps, none other of her sex ever did—that the bold black eyes of this fine

gentleman were in reality of a brownish and even
tender grey.

There was a small garden before a white cottage
in a side-street, that attracted Mr. Oakhurst's
attention. It was filled with roses, heliotrope, and
verbena—flowers familiar enough to him in the
expensive and more portable form of bouquets,
but, as it seemed to him then, never before so
notably lovely. Perhaps it was because the dew
was yet fresh upon them ; perhaps it was because
they were únplucked : but Mr. Oakhurst admired
them—not as a possible future tribute to the fascinating and accomplished Miss Ethelinda, then performing at the Varieties, for Mr. Oakhurst's especial
benefit, as she had often assured him ; nor yet as a
douceur to the inthralling Miss Montmorrissy, with
whom Mr. Oakhurst expected to sup that evening ;
but simply for himself, and, mayhap, for the flowers'
sake. Howbeit he passed on, and so out into the
open Plaza, where, finding a bench under a cotton-
wood-tree, he first dusted the seat with his handkerchief, and then sat down.

It was a fine morning. The air was so still and
calm that a sigh from the sycamores seemed like
the deep-drawn breath of the just awakening tree,
and the faint rustle of its boughs as the outstretch-
ing of cramped and reviving limbs. Far away the
Sierras stood out against a sky so remote as to be
of no possible colour—so remote that even the sun
despaired of ever reaching it, and so expended its

strength recklessly on the whole landscape, until it fairly glittered in a white and vivid contrast. With a very rare impulse, Mr. Oakhurst took off his hat, and half reclined on the bench, with his face to the sky. Certain birds who had taken a critical attitude on a spray above him, apparently began an animated discussion regarding his possible malevolent intentions. One or two, emboldened by the silence, hopped on the ground at his feet, until the sound of wheels on the gravel walk frightened them away.

Looking up, he saw a man coming slowly towards him, wheeling a nondescript vehicle, in which a woman was partly sitting, partly reclining. Without knowing why, Mr. Oakhurst instantly conceived that the carriage was the invention and workmanship of the man, partly from its oddity, partly from the strong, mechanical hand that grasped it, and partly from a certain pride and visible consciousness in the manner in which the man handled it. Then Mr. Oakhurst saw something more: the man's face was familiar. With that regal faculty of not forgetting a face that had ever given him professional audience, he instantly classified it under the following mental formula: "At 'Frisco, Polka Saloon. Lost his week's wages, I reckon—seventy dollars—on red. Never came again." There was, however, no trace of this in the calm eyes and unmoved face that he turned upon the stranger, who, on the contrary, blushed,

looked embarrassed, hesitated, and then stopped
with an involuntary motion that brought the carriage and its fair occupant face to face with Mr.
Oakhurst.

I should hardly do justice to the position she
will occupy in this veracious chronicle by describing
the lady now, if, indeed, I am able to do it at
all. Certainly the popular estimate was conflict-
ing. The late Colonel Starbottle —to whose large
experience of a charming sex I have before been
indebted for many valuable suggestions—had, I
regret to say, depreciated her fascinations. "A
yellow-faced cripple, by dash! a sick woman, with
mahogany eyes ; one of your blanked spiritual
creatures—with no flesh on her bones." On the
other hand, however, she enjoyed later much com-
plimentary disparagement from her own sex. Miss
Celestina Howard, second leader in the *ballet* at
the Varieties, had, with great alliterative directness, in after-years, denominated her as an "aquiline asp." Mdlle. Brimborion remembered that she
had always warned "Mr. Jack" that this woman
would "empoison" him. But Mr. Oakhurst, whose
impressions are, perhaps, the most important, only
saw a pale, thin, deep-eyed woman, raised above
the level of her companion by the refinement of
long suffering and isolation, and a certain shy virginity of manner. There was a suggestion of
physical purity in the folds of her fresh-looking
robe, and a certain picturesque tastefulness in the

details, that, without knowing why, made him think that the robe was her invention and handiwork, even as the carriage she occupied was evidently the work of her companion. Her own hand, a trifle too thin, but well-shaped, subtle-fingered, and gentlewomanly, rested on the side of the carriage, the counterpart of the strong mechanical grasp of her companion's.

There was some obstruction to the progress of the vehicle ; and Mr. Oakhurst stepped forward to assist. While the wheel was being lifted over the curbstone, it was necessary that she should hold his arm ; and for a moment her thin hand rested there, light and cold as a snow-flake, and then, as it seemed to him, like a snow-flake melted away. Then there was a pause, and then conversation, the lady joining occasionally and shyly.

It appeared that they were man and wife ; that for the past two years she had been a great invalid, and had lost the use of her lower limbs from rheumatism ; that until lately she had been confined to her bed, until her husband—who was a master carpenter—had bethought himself to make her this carriage. He took her out regularly for an airing before going to work, because it was his only time, and—they attracted less attention. They had tried many doctors, but without avail. They had been advised to go to the Sulphur Springs : but it was expensive. Mr. Decker, the husband, had once saved eighty dollars for that purpose, but while in San Francisco had his pocket picked—Mr. Decker was so senseless ! (The intelligent reader need not be told that it is the lady who is speaking.) They had never been able to make up the sum again, and they had given up the idea. It was a dreadful thing to have one's pocket picked. Did he not think so ?

Her husband's face was crimson ; but Mr. Oakhurst's countenance was quite calm and unmoved, as he gravely agreed with her, and walked by her side until they passed the little garden that he had admired. Here Mr. Oakhurst commanded a halt, and, going to the door, astounded the proprietor by a preposterously extravagant offer for a choice of the flowers. Presently he returned to the carriage with his arms full of roses, heliotrope, and verbena, and cast them in the lap of the invalid. While she was bending over them with childish delight, Mr. Oakhurst took the opportunity of drawing her husband aside.

" Perhaps," he said, in a low voice, and a manner quite free from any personal annoyance—"perhaps it's just as well that you lied to her as you did. You can say now that the pickpocket was arrested the other day, and you got your money back." Mr. Oakhurst quietly slipped four twenty-dollar gold pieces into the broad hand of the bewildered Mr. Decker. " Say that—or anything you like—but the truth. Promise me you won't say that."

The man promised. Mr. Oakhurst quietly returned to the front of the little carriage. The
sick woman was still eagerly occupied with the
flowers, and, as she raised her eyes to his, her
faded cheek seemed to have caught some colour
from the roses, and her eyes some of their dewy
freshness. But at that instant Mr. Oakhurst lifted
his hat, and before she could thank him was
gone.

I grieve to say that Mr. Decker shamelessly
broke his promise. That night, in the very goodness of his heart and uxorious self-abnegation, he,
like all devoted husbands, not only offered himself,
but his friend and benefactor, as a sacrifice on the
family altar. It is only fair, however, to add that
he spoke with great fervour of the generosity of
Mr. Oakhurst, and dwelt with an enthusiasm quite
common with his class on the mysterious fame and
prodigal vices of the gambler.

"And now, Elsie dear, say that you'll forgive
me," said Mr. Decker, dropping on one knee beside
his wife's couch. "I did it for the best. It was
for you, dearey, that I put that money on them
cards that night in 'Frisco. I thought to win a
heap—enough to take you away, and enough left
to get you a new dress."

Mrs. Decker smiled, and pressed her husband's
hand. "I do forgive you, Joe dear," she said, still
smiling, with eyes abstractedly fixed on the ceiling;
"and you ought to be whipped for deceiving me

so, you bad boy! and making me make such a speech. There, say no more about it. If you'll be very good hereafter, and will just now hand me that cluster of roses, I'll forgive you." She took the branch in her fingers, lifted the roses to her face, and presently said, behind their leaves—

" Joe ! "

" What is it, lovey ? "

" Do you think that this Mr: — what do you call him?—Jack Oakhurst would have given that money back to you, if I hadn't made that speech ? "

" Yes."

" If he hadn't seen me at all ? "

Mr. Decker looked up. His wife had managed in some way to cover up her whole face with the roses, except her eyes, which were dangerously bright.

"'No ! It was you, Elsie—it was all along of seeing you that made him do it."

A poor sick woman like me ? "

" A sweet, little, lovely, pooty Elsie—Joe's own little wifey ! How could he help it ? "

Mrs. Decker fondly cast one arm around her husband's neck, still keeping the roses to her face with the other. From behind them she began to murmur gently and idiotically, " Dear, ole square Joey. Elsie's oney booful big bear." But, really, I do not see that my duty as a chronicler of facts compels me to continue this little lady's speech any further ; and, out of respect to the unmarried reader, I stop.

Nevertheless, the next morning Mrs. Decker betrayed some slight and apparently uncalled for irritability on reaching the Plaza, and presently desired her husband to wheel her back home. Moreover, she was very much astonished at meeting Mr. Oakhurst just as they were returning, and even doubted if it were he, and questioned her husband as to his identity with the stranger of yesterday as he approached. Her manner to Mr. Oakhurst, also, was quite in contrast with her husband's frank welcome. Mr. Oakhurst instantly detected it. "Her husband has told her all, and she dislikes me," he said to himself, with that fatal appreciation of the half-truths of a woman's motives that causes the wisest masculine critic to stumble. He lingered only long enough to take the business address of the husband, and then lifting his hat gravely, without looking at the lady, went his way. It struck the honest master-carpenter as one of the charming anomalies of his wife's character, that, although the meeting was evidently very much constrained and unpleasant, instantly afterwards his wife's spirits began to rise. "You was hard on him, a leetle hard; wasn't you, Elsie?" said Mr. Decker, deprecatingly. "I'm afraid he may think I've broke my promise."—"Ah, indeed!" said the lady, indifferently. Mr. Decker instantly stepped round to the front of the vehicle. "You look like an A 1 first-class lady riding down Broadway in her own carriage, Elsie," said he. "I never seed you lookin' so peart and sassy before."

A few days later, the proprietor of the San Isabel Sulphur Springs received the following note in Mr. Oakhurst's well-known dainty hand :—

"DEAR STEVE,—I've been thinking over your proposition to buy Nichols's quarter interest, and have concluded to go in.   But I don't see how the thing will pay until you have more accommodation down there, and for the best class—I mean *my* customers.   What we want is an extension to the main building, and two or three cottages put up.   I send down a builder to take hold of the job at once.   He takes his sick wife with him; and you are to look after them as you would for one of us.

"I may run down there myself after the races, just to look after things ; but I sha'n't set up any game this season.
        "Yours always,   "JOHN OAKHURST."

It was only the last sentence of this letter that provoked criticism.   "I can understand," said Mr. Hamlin, a professional brother, to whom Mr. Oakhurst's letter was shown—"I can understand why Jack goes in heavy and builds ; for it's a sure spec, and is bound to be a mighty soft thing in time, if he comes here regularly.   But why in blank he don't set up a bank this season, and take the chance of getting some of the money back that he puts into circulation in building, is what gets me.   I wonder now," he mused deeply, "what *is* his little game."

The season had been a prosperous one to Mr. Oakhurst, and proportionally disastrous to several members of the legislature, judges, colonels, and others who had enjoyed but briefly the pleasure of Mr. Oakhurst's midnight society.   And yet Sacramento had become very dull to him. He had lately formed a habit of early morning walks, so unusual and startling to his friends, both male and female, as to occasion the intensest curiosity. Two or three of the latter set spies upon his track; but the inquisition resulted only in the discovery that Mr. Oakhurst walked to the Plaza, sat down upon one particular bench for a few moments, and then returned without seeing anybody; and the theory that there was a woman in the case was abandoned. A few superstitious gentlemen of his own profession believed that he did it for "luck." Some others, more practical, declared that he went out to "study points."

After the races at Marysville, Mr. Oakhurst went to San Francisco; from that place he returned to Marysville, but a few days after was seen at San José, Santa Cruz, and Oakland. Those who met him declared that his manner was restless and feverish, and quite unlike his ordinary calmness and phlegm. Col. Starbottle pointed out the fact, that at San Francisco, at the club, Jack had declined to deal. "Hand shaky, sir; depend upon it. Don t stimulate enough—blank him!"

From San José he started to go to Oregon by land, with a rather expensive outfit of horses and camp equipage; but, on reaching Stockton, he suddenly diverged, and four hours later found him with a single horse entering the cañon of the San Isabel Warm Sulphur Springs.

It was a pretty triangular valley, lying at the
foot of three sloping mountains, dark with pines,
and fantastic with mandrono and manzanita. Nestling against the mountain-side, the straggling
buildings and long piazza of the hotel glittered
through the leaves, and here and there shone a
white toy-like cottage. Mr. Oakhurst was not an
admirer of Nature ; but he felt something of the
same novel satisfaction in the view, that he expe-
rienced in his first morning-walk in Sacramento.
And now carriages began to pass him on the road,
filled with gaily-dressed women ; and the cold
California outlines of the landscape began to take
upon themselves somewhat of a human warmth and
colour. And then the long hotel piazza came in
view, efflorescent with the full-toiletted fair. Mr.
Oakhurst, a good rider after the California fashion,
did not check his speed as he approached ·his des-
tination, but charged the hotel at a gallop, threw
his horse on his haunches within a foot of the
piazza, and then quietly emerged from the cloud of
dust that veiled his dismounting.

Whatever feverish excitement might have raged
within, all his habitual calm returned as he stepped
upon the piazza. With the instinct of long habit,
he turned and faced the battery of eyes with the
same cold indifference with which he had for years
encountered the half-hidden sneers of men and the
half-frightened admiration of women. Only one
person stepped forward to welcome him. Oddly

enough it was Dick Hamilton, perhaps the only one present who, by birth, education, and position, might have satisfied the most fastidious social critic. Happily for Mr. Oakhurst's reputation, he was also a very rich banker and social leader. "Do you know who that is you spoke to?" asked young Parker, with an alarmed expression. "Yes," replied Hamilton, with characteristic effrontery. "The man you lost a thousand dollars to last week. *I* only know him *socially*." "But isn't he a gambler?" queried the youngest Miss Smith. "He is," replied Hamilton; "but I wish, my dear young lady, that we all played as open and honest a game as our friend yonder, and were as willing as he is to abide by its fortunes."

But Mr. Oakhurst was happily out of hearing of this colloquy, and was even then lounging listlessly yet watchfully along the upper hall. Suddenly he heard a light footstep behind him, and then his name called in a familiar voice that drew the blood quickly to his heart. He turned, and she stood before him.

But how transformed! If I have hesitated to describe the hollow-eyed cripple, the quaintly-dressed artizan's wife, a few pages ago, what shall I do with this graceful, shapely, elegantly-attired gentlewoman into whom she has been merged within these two months? In good faith she was very pretty. You and I, my dear madam, would have been quick to see that those charming dimples

were misplaced for true beauty, and too fixed in
their quality for honest mirthfulness; that the delicate lines around these aquiline nostrils were cruel
and selfish; that the sweet virginal surprise of these
lovely eyes were as apt to be opened on her plate
as upon the gallant speeches of her dinner partner;
that her sympathetic colour came and went more
with her own spirits than yours. But you and I
are not in love with her, dear madam, and Mr.
Oakhurst is. And, even in the folds of her Parisian
gown, I am afraid this poor fellow saw the same
subtle strokes of purity that he had seen in her
homespun robe. And then there was the delight-
ful revelation that she could walk, and that she had
dear little feet of her own in the tiniest slippers of
her French shoemaker, with such preposterous blue
bows, and Chappell's own stamp—Rue de something or other, Paris—on the narrow sole.

He ran towards her with a heightened colour and
outstretched hands. But she whipped her own
behind her, glanced rapidly up and down the long
hall, and stood looking at him with a half-audacious,
half-mischievous admiration, in utter contrast to
her old reserve.

" I've a great mind not to shake hands with you
at all. You passed me just now on the piazza
without speaking; and I ran after you, as I suppose many another poor woman has done."

Mr. Oakhurst stammered that she was so
changed.

"The more reason why you should know me. Who changed me? You. You have re-created me. You found a helpless, crippled, sick, poverty-stricken woman, with one dress to her back, and that her own make, and you gave her life, health, strength, and fortune. You did; and you know it, sir. How do you like your work?" She caught the side-seams of her gown in either hand, and dropped him a playful courtesy. Then, with a sudden, relenting gesture, she gave him both her hands.

Outrageous as this speech was, and unfeminine as I trust every fair reader will deem it, I fear it pleased Mr. Oakhurst. Not but that he was accustomed to a certain frank female admiration; but then it was of the *coulisse*, and not of the cloister with which he always persisted in associating Mrs. Decker. To be addressed in this way by an invalid Puritan, a sick saint with the austerity of suffering still clothing her, a woman who had a Bible on the dressing-table, who went to church three times a day, and was devoted to her husband, completely bowled him over. He still held her hands as she went on—

"Why didn't you come before? What were you doing in Marysville, in San José, in Oakland? You see I have followed you. I saw you as you came down the cañon, and knew you at once. I saw your letter to Joseph, and knew you were coming. Why didn't you write to me? You will some time!—Good evening, Mr. Hamilton."

She had withdrawn her hands, but not until Hamilton, ascending the staircase, was nearly abreast of them. He raised his hat to her with well-bred composure, nodded familiarly to Oakhurst, and passed on. When he had gone, Mrs. Decker lifted her eyes to Mr. Oakhurst. "Some day I shall ask a great favour of you."

Mr. Oakkurst begged that it should be now. "No, not until you know me better. Then, some day, I shall want you to—kill that man!"

She laughed such a pleasant little ringing laugh, such a display of dimples—albeit a little fixed in the corners of her mouth—such an innocent light in her brown eyes, and such a lovely colour in her cheeks, that Mr. Oakhurst (who seldom laughed) was fain to laugh too. It was as if a lamb had proposed to a fox a foray into a neighbouring sheepfold.

A few evenings after this, Mrs. Decker arose from a charmed circle of her admirers on the hotel piazza, excused herself for a few moments, laughingly declined an escort, and ran over to her little cottage—one of her husband's creation—across the road. Perhaps from the sudden and unwonted exercise in her still convalescent state, she breathed hurriedly and feverishly as she entered her boudoir, and once or twice placed her hand upon her breast. She was startled on turning up the light to find her husband lying on the sofa.

"You look hot and excited, Elsie, love," said Mr. Decker. "You ain't took worse, are you?"

G

Mrs. Decker's face had paled, but now flushed again. " No," she said ; " only a little pain here," as she again placed her hand upon her corsage.

" Can I do anything for you ? " said Mr. Decker, rising with affectionate concern.

" Run over to the hotel and get me some brandy, quick ! "

Mr. Decker ran. Mrs. Decker closed and bolted the door, and then, putting her hand to her bosom, drew out the pain. It was folded foursquare, and was, I grieve to say, in Mr. Oakhurst's handwriting.

She devoured it with burning eyes and cheeks until there came a step upon the porch ; then she hurriedly replaced it in her bosom, and unbolted the door. Her husband entered. She raised the spirits to her lips, and declared herself better.

" Are you going over there again to-night ? " asked Mr. Decker, submissively.

" No," said Mrs. Decker, with her eyes fixed dreamily on the floor.

" I wouldn't if I was you," said Mr. Decker, with a sigh of relief. After a pause, he took a seat on the sofa, and, drawing his wife to his side, said, " Do you know what I was thinking of when you came in, Elsie ? " Mrs. Decker ran her fingers through his stiff black hair, and couldn't imagine.

" I was thinking of old times, Elsie : I was thinking of the days when I built that kerridge for y'ou, Elsie—when I used to take you out to ride, and was both hoss and driver. We was poor then, and you was sick, Elsie ; but we was happy. We've got money now, and a house ; and you're quite another woman. I may say, dear, that you're a *new* woman. And that's where the trouble comes in. I could build you a kerridge, Elsie ; I could build you a house, Elsie—but there I stopped. I couldn't build up *you*. You're strong and pretty, Elsie, and fresh and new. But somehow, Elsie, you ain't no work of mine ! "

He paused. With one hand laid gently on his forehead, and the other pressed upon her bosom, as if to feel certain of the presence of her pain, she said sweetly and soothingly

" But it was your work, dear."

Mr. Decker shook his head sorrowfully. " No, Elsie, not mine. I had the chance to do it once, and I let it go. It's done now—but not by me."

Mrs. Decker raised her surprised, innocent eyes to his. He kissed her tenderly, and then went on in a more cheerful voice—

" That ain't all I was thinking of, Elsie. I was thinking that maybe you give too much of your company to that Mr. Hamilton. Not that there's any wrong in it, to you or him ; but it might make people talk. You're the only one here, Elsie," said the master-carpenter, looking fondly at his wife "who isn't talked about, whose work ain't inspected or condemned."

Mrs. Decker was glad he had spoken about it. She had thought so too. But she could not well be uncivil to Mr. Hamilton, who was a fine gentleman, without making a powerful enemy. "And he's always treated me as if I was a born lady in his own circle," added the little woman, with a certain pride that made her husband fondly smile. "But I have thought of a plan. He will not stay here if I should go away. If, for instance, I went to San Francisco to visit ma for a few days, he would be gone before I should return."

Mr. Decker was delighted. "By all means," he said, "go to-morrow. Jack Oakhurst is going down ; and I'll put you in his charge."

Mrs. Decker did not think it was prudent. "Mr. Oakhurst is our friend, Joseph ; but you know his reputation." In fact she did not know that she ought to go now, knowing that he was going the same day ; but, with a kiss, Mr. Decker overcame her scruples. She yielded gracefully. Few women, in fact, knew how to give up a point as charmingly as she.

She stayed a week in San Francisco. When she returned she was a trifle thinner and paler than she had been. This she explained as the result of perhaps too active exercise and excitement. "I was out of doors nearly all the time, as ma will tell you," she said to her husband, "and always alone. I am getting quite independent now," she added gaily. "I don't want any escort. I believe,

Joey dear, I could get along even without you, I'm so brave!"

But her visit, apparently, had not been productive of her impelling design. Mr. Hamilton had not gone, but had remained, and called upon them that very evening. "I've thought of a plan, Joey dear," said Mrs. Decker, when he had departed. " Poor Mr. Oakhurst has a miserable room at the hotel. Suppose you ask him, when he returns from San Francisco, to stop with us. He can have our spare room. "I don't think," she added archly, " that Mr. Hamilton will call often." Her husband laughed, intimated that she was a little coquette, pinched her cheek, and complied. "The queer thing about a woman," he said afterwards confidentially to Mr. Oakhurst, " is, that, without having any plan of her own, she'll take anybody's, and build a house on it entirely different to suit herself. And dern my skin if you'll be able to say whether or not you didn't give the scale and measurements yourself! That's what gets me!"

The next week Mr. Oakhurst was installed in the Deckers' cottage. The business relations of her husband and himself were known to all, and her own reputation was above suspicion. Indeed, few women were more popular. She was domestic, she was prudent, she was pious. In a country of great feminine freedom and latitude, she never rode or walked with anybody but her husband. In an epoch of slang and ambiguous expression, she was always precise, and formal in her speech. In the midst of a fashion of ostentatious decoration, she never wore a diamond, nor a single valuable jewel. She never permitted an indecorum in public. She never countenanced the familiarities of Californian society. She declaimed against the prevailing tone of infidelity and scepticism in religion. Few people who were present will ever forget the dignified yet stately manner with which she rebuked Mr. Hamilton in the public parlour for entering upon the discussion of a work on materialism, lately published ; and some among them, also, will not forget the expression of amused surprise on Mr. Hamilton's face, that gradually changed to sardonic gravity, as he courteously waived his point ; certainly not Mr. Oakhurst, who, from that moment, began to be uneasily impatient of his friend, and even—if such a term could be applied to any moral quality in Mr. Oakhurst—to fear him.

For during this time Mr. Oakhurst had begun to show symptoms of a change in his usual habits. He was seldom, if ever, seen in his old haunts, in a bar-room, or with his old associates. Pink and white notes, in distracted handwriting, accumulated on the dressing-table in his rooms at Sacramento. It was given out in San Francisco that he had some organic disease of the heart, for which his physician had prescribed perfect rest. He read more ; he took long walks ; he sold his fast horses ; he went to church.

I have a very vivid recollection of his first appearance there. He did not accompany the Deckers, nor did he go into their pew, but came in as the service commenced, and took a seat quietly in one of the back pews. By some mysterious instinct, his presence became presently known to the congregation, some of whom so far forgot themselves, in their curiosity, as to face around, and apparently address their responses to him. Before the service was over, it was pretty well understood that "miserable sinners" meant Mr. Oakhurst. Nor did this mysterious influence fail to affect the officiating clergyman, who introduced an allusion to Mr. Oakhurst's calling and habits in a sermon on the architecture of Solomon's temple, and in a manner so pointed, and yet laboured, as to cause the youngest of us to flame with indignation. Happily, however, it was lost upon Jack: I do not think he even heard it. His handsome, colourless face, albeit a trifle worn and thoughtful, was inscrutable. Only once, during the singing of a hymn, at a certain note in the contralto's voice, there crept into his dark eyes a look of wistful tenderness, so yearning and yet so hopeless, that those who were watching him felt their own glisten. Yet I retain a very vivid remembrance of his standing up to receive the benediction with the suggestion, in his manner and tightly-buttoned coat, of taking the fire of his adversary at ten paces. After church, he disappeared as quietly as he had entered, and fortunately escaped hearing the comments on his rash act. His appearance was generally considered as an impertinence, attributable only to some wanton fancy, or possibly a bet. One or two thought that the sexton was exceedingly remiss in not turning him out after discovering who he was; and a prominent pewholder remarked, that if he couldn't take his wife and daughters to that church, without exposing them to such an influence, he would try to find some church where he could. Another traced Mr. Oakhurst's presence to certain Broad Church radical tendencies, which he regretted to say he had lately noted in their pastor. Deacon Sawyer, whose delicately-organized, sickly wife had already borne him eleven children, and died in an ambitious attempt to complete the dozen, avowed that the presence of a person of Mr. Oakhurst's various and indiscriminate gallantries was an insult to the memory of the deceased, that, as a man, he could not brook.

It was about this time that Mr. Oakhurst, contrasting himself with a conventional world in which he had hitherto rarely mingled, became aware that there was something in his face, figure, and carriage quite unlike other men—something that, if it did not betray his former career, at least showed an individuality and originality that was suspicious. In this belief, he shaved off his long, silken, moustache, and religiously brushed out his cluster-

ing curls every morning. He even went so far as
to affect a negligence of dress, and hid his small,
slim, arched feet in the largest and heaviest walking-
shoes. There is a story told that he went to his
tailor in Sacramento, and asked him to make him
a suit of clothes like everybody else. The tailor,
familiar with Mr. Oakhurst's fastidiousness, did
not know what he meant. " I mean," said Mr.
Oakhurst savagely, "something *respectable*,—something that doesn't exactly fit me, you know." But,
however Mr. Oakhurst might hide his shapely
limbs in homespun and home-made garments, there
was something in his carriage, something in the
pose of his beautiful head, something in the strong
and fine manliness of his presence, something in
the perfect and utter discipline and control of his
muscles, something in the high repose of his
nature—a repose not so much a matter of intel-
lectual ruling as of his very nature—that, go where
he would, and with whom, he was always a notable
man in ten thousand. Perhaps this was never so
clearly intimated to Mr. Oakhurst, as when, emboldened by Mr. Hamilton's advice and assistance,
and his own predilections, he became a San
Francisco broker. Even before objection was made
to his presence in the Board—the objection, I
remember, was urged very eloquently by Watt
Sanders, who was supposed to be the inventor of the
" freezing-out " system of disposing of poor stockholders, and who also enjoyed the reputation of

having been the impelling cause of Briggs of Tuolumne's ruin and suicide—even before this formal
protest of respectability against lawlessness, the
aquiline suggestions of Mr. Oakhurst's mien and
countenance, not only prematurely fluttered the
pigeons, but absolutely occasioned much uneasiness among the fish-hawks who circled below him
with their booty. "Dash me ! but he's as likely to
go after us as anybody," said Joe Fielding.

It wanted but a few days before the close of the
brief summer season at San Isabel Warm Springs.
Already there had been some migration of the
more fashionable ; and there was an uncomfortable
suggestion of dregs and lees in the social life that
remained. Mr. Oakhurst was moody. It was
hinted that even the secure reputation of Mrs.
Decker could no longer protect her from the gossip
which his presence excited. It is but fair to her to
say, that, during the last few weeks of this trying
ordeal she looked like a sweet, pale martyr, and
conducted herself towards her traducers with the
gentle, forgiving manner of one who relied not
upon the idle homage of the crowd, but upon the
security of a principle that was dearer than popular
favour. "They talk about myself and Mr. Oakhurst, my dear," she said to a friend ; " but heaven
and my husband can best answer their calumny.
It never shall be said that my husband ever turned
his back upon a friend in the moment of his ad-

versity, because the position was changed—because his friend was poor, and he was rich." This was the first intimation to the public that Jack had lost money, although it was known generally that the Deckers had lately bought some valuable property in San Francisco.

A few evenings after this, an incident occurred which seemed to unpleasantly discord with the general social harmony that had always existed at San Isabel. It was at dinner ; and Mr. Oakhurst and Mr. Hamilton, who sat together at a separate table, were observed to rise in some agitation. When they reached the hall, by a common instinct they stepped into a little breakfast-room which was vacant, and closed the door. Then Mr. Hamilton turned with a half-amused, half-serious smile towards his friend, and said—

" If we are to quarrel, Jack Oakhurst—you and I —in the name of all that is ridiculous, don't let it be about a ——"

I do not know what was the epithet intended. It was either unspoken or lost ; for at that very instant Mr. Oakhurst raised a wineglass, and dashed its contents into Hamilton's face.

· As they faced each other, the men seemed to have changed natures. Mr. Oakhurst was trembling with excitement, and the wineglass that he returned to the table shivered between his fingers. Mr. Hamilton stood there, greyish white, erect, and dripping. After a pause, he said coldly—

"So be it. But remember, our quarrel commences here. If I fall by your hand, you shall not use it to clear her character: if you fall by mine, you shall not be called a martyr. I am sorry it has come to this; but amen, the sooner now, the better."

He turned proudly, dropped his lids over his cold steel-blue eyes, as if sheathing a rapier, bowed, and passed coldly out.

They met, twelve hours later, in a little hollow two miles from the hotel, on the Stockton road. As Mr. Oakhurst received his pistol from Col. Starbottle's hands, he said to him in a low voice, "Whatever turns up or down, I shall not return to the hotel. You will find some directions in my room. Go there—." But his voice suddenly faltered, and he turned his glistening eyes away, to his second's intense astonishment. "I've been out a dozen times with Jack Oakhurst," said Col. Starbottle afterwards, " and I never saw him anyways cut before. Blank me if I didn't think he was losing his sand, till he walked to position."

The two reports were almost simultaneous. Mr. Oakhurst's right arm dropped suddenly to his side, and his pistol would have fallen from his paralyzed fingers; but the discipline of trained nerve and muscle prevailed, and he kept his grasp until he had shifted it to the other hand, without changing his position. Then there was a silence that seemed interminable, a gathering of two or three dark figures where a smoke-curl still lazily floated, and then the hurried, husky, panting voice of Col. Starbottle in his ear, "He's hit hard— through the lungs—you must run for it!"

Jack turned his dark, questioning eyes upon his second, but did not seem to listen—rather seemed to hear some other voice, remoter in the distance. He hesitated, and then made a step forward in the direction of the distant group. Then he paused again as the figures separated, and the surgeon came hastily towards him.

"He would like to speak with you a moment," said the man. "You have little time to lose, I know; but," he added in a lower voice, "it is my duty to tell you he has still less."

A look of despair, so hopeless in its intensity, swept over Mr. Oakhurst's usually impassive face, that the surgeon started. "You are hit," he said, glancing at Jack's helpless arm.

"Nothing—a mere scratch," said Jack, hastily. Then he added with a bitter laugh, "I'm not in luck to-day. But come: we'll see what he wants."

His long, feverish stride outstripped the surgeon's, and in another moment he stood where the dying man lay—like most dying men—the one calm, composed, central figure of an anxious group. Mr. Oakhurst's face was less calm as he dropped on one knee beside him, and took his hand. "I want to speak with this gentleman alone," said Hamilton, with something of his old imperious manner, as he turned to those about him. When they drew back, he looked up in Oakhurst's face.

"I've something to tell you, Jack."

His own face was white, but not so white as that which Mr. Oakhurst bent over him—a face so ghastly, with haunting doubts, and a hopeless presentiment of coming evil—a face so piteous in its infinite weariness and envy of death, that the dying man was touched, even in the languor of dissolution, with a pang of compassion; and the cynical smile faded from his lips.

"Forgive me, Jack," he whispered more feebly, "for what I have to say. I don't say it in anger, but only because it must be said. I could not do my duty to you, I could not die contented, until you knew it all. It's a miserable business at best, all round. But it can't be helped now. Only I ought to have fallen by Decker's pistol, and not yours."

A flush like fire came into Jack's cheek, and he would have risen; but Hamilton held him fast.

"Listen! In my pocket you will find two letters. Take them—there! You will know the handwriting. But promise you will not read them until you are in a place of safety. Promise me."

Jack did not speak, but held the letters between his fingers as if they had been burning coals.

"Promise me," said Hamilton, faintly.

"Why?" asked Oakhurst, dropping his friend's hand coldly.

"Because," said the dying man, with a bitter smile—"because—when you have read them—you—will—go back—to capture—and death!"

They were his last words. He pressed Jack's hand faintly. Then his grasp relaxed, and he fell back a corpse.

It was nearly ten o'clock at night, and Mrs. Decker reclined languidly upon the sofa with a novel in her hand, while her husband discussed the politics of the country in the bar-room of the hotel. It was a warm night; and the French window looking out upon a little balcony was partly open. Suddenly she heard a foot upon the balcony, and she raised her eyes from the book with a slight start. The next moment the window was hurriedly thrust wide, and a man entered.

Mrs. Decker rose to her feet with a little cry of alarm.

"For Heaven's sake, Jack, are you mad? He has only gone for a little while—he may return at any moment. Come an hour later, to-morrow, any time when I can get rid of him—but go, now, dear, at once."

Mr. Oakhurst walked towards the door, bolted it, and then faced her without a word. His face was haggard; his coat-sleeve hung loosely over an arm that was bandaged and bloody.

Nevertheless her voice did not falter as she turned again towards him. "What has happened, Jack? Why are you here?"

He opened his coat, and threw two letters in her lap.

"To return your lover's letters; to kill you— and then myself," he said, in a voice so low as to almost inaudible.

Among the many virtues of this admirable woman was invincible courage. She did not faint; she did not cry out; she sat quietly down again, folded her hands in her lap, and said calmly—

"And why should you not?"

Had she recoiled, had she shown any fear or contrition, had she essayed an explanation or apology, Mr. Oakhurst would have looked upon it as an evidence of guilt. But there is no quality that courage recognizes so quickly as courage. There is no condition that desperation bows before but desperation. And Mr. Oakhurst's power of analysis was not so keen as to prevent him from confounding her courage with a moral quality. Even in his fury, he could not help admiring this dauntless invalid.

"Why should you not?" she repeated, with a smile. "You gave me life, health, and happiness, Jack. You gave me your love. Why should you not take what you have given? Go on. I am ready."

She held out her hands with that same infinite grace of yielding with which she had taken his own on the first day of their meeting at the hotel. Jack raised his head, looked at her for one wild moment, dropped upon his knees beside her, and raised the folds of her dress to his feverish lips. But she was too clever not to instantly see her victory : she was too much of a woman, with all her cleverness, to refrain from pressing that victory home. At the same moment, as with the impulse of an outraged and wounded woman, she rose, and, with an imperious gesture, pointed to the window. Mr. Oakhurst rose in his turn, cast one glance upon her, and without another word passed out of her presence for ever.

When he had gone, she closed the window and bolted it, and, going to the chimney-piece, placed the letters, one by one, in the flame of the candle until they were consumed. I would not have the reader think that, during this painful operation, she was unmoved. Her hand trembled, and—not being a brute—for some minutes (perhaps longer) she felt very badly, and the corners of her sensitive mouth were depressed. When her husband arrived, it was with a genuine joy that she ran to him, and nestled against his broad breast with a feeling of security that thrilled the honest fellow to the core.

" But I've heard dreadful news to-night, Elsie," said Mr. Decker, after a few endearments were exchanged.

" Don't tell me anything dreadful, dear : I'm not well to-night," she pleaded, sweetly.

" But it's about Mr. Oakhurst and Hamilton."

"Please !" Mr. Decker could not resist the

H

petitionary grace of those white hands and that sensitive mouth, and took her to his arms. Suddenly he said, " What's that ? "

He was pointing to the bosom of her white dress. Where Mr. Oakhurst had touched her there was a spot of blood.

It was nothing : she had slightly cut her hand in closing the window ; it shut so hard ! If Mr. Decker had remembered to close and bolt the shutter before he went out, he might have saved her this. There was such a genuine irritability and force in this remark that Mr. Decker was quite overcome by remorse. But Mrs. Decker forgave him with that graciousness which I have before pointed out in these pages. And with the halo of that forgiveness and marital confidence still lingering above the pair, we will leave them, and return to Mr. Oakhurst.

But not for two weeks. At the end of that time, he walked into his rooms in Sacramento, and in his old manner took his seat at the faro-table.

" How's your arm, Jack ? " asked an incautious player.

There was a smile followed the question, which, however, ceased as Jack looked up quietly at the speaker.

" It bothers my dealing a little ; but I can shoot as well with my left."

The game was continued in that decorous silence which usually distinguished the table at which Mr John Oakhurst presided.

HOW OLD MAN PLUNKETT WENT
HOME.

I THINK we all loved him. Even after he mismanaged the affairs of the Amity Ditch Company we commiserated him, although most of us were stockholders, and lost heavily. I remember that the blacksmith went so far as to say that "them chaps as put that responsibility on the old man oughter be lynched." But the blacksmith was not a stockholder; and the expression was looked upon as the excusable extravagance of a large, sympathizing nature, that, when combined with a powerful frame, was unworthy of notice. At least, that was the way they put it. Yet I think there was a general feeling of regret that this misfortune would interfere with the old man's long-cherished plan of "going home."

Indeed, for the last ten years he had been "going home." He was going home after a six months' sojourn at Monte Flat; he was going home after the first rains; he was going home when the rains were over; he was going home when he had cut the timber on Buckeye Hill, when there was pasture on Dow's Flat, when he struck pay-dirt on Eureka

Hill, when the Amity Company paid its first dividend, when the election was over, when he had received an answer from his wife. And so the years rolled by, the spring rains came and went, the woods of Buckeye Hill were level with the ground, the pasture on Dow's Flat grew sear and dry, Eureka Hill yielded its pay-dirt and swamped its owner, the first dividends of the Amity Company were made from the assessments of stockholders, there were new county officers at Monte Flat, his wife's answer had changed into a persistent question, and still old man Plunkett remained.

It is only fair to say that he had made several distinct essays towards going. Five years before, he had bidden good-bye to Monte Hill with much effusion and hand-shaking. But he never got any farther than the next town. Here he was induced to trade the sorrel colt he was riding for a bay mare—a transaction that at once opened to his lively fancy a vista of vast and successful future speculation. A few days after, Abner Dean of Angel's received a letter from him, stating that he was going to Visalia to buy horses. "I am satisfied," wrote Plunkett, with that elevated rhetoric for which his correspondence was remarkable—"I am satisfied that we are at last developing the real resources of California. The world will yet look to Dow's Flat as the great stock-raising centre. In view of the interests involved, I have deferred my departure for a month." It was two before he again returned to us—penniless. Six months later, he was again enabled to start for the Eastern States ; and this time he got as far as San Francisco. I have before me a letter which I received a few days after his arrival, from which I venture to give an extract : "You know, my dear boy, that I have always believed that gambling, as it is absurdly called, is still in its infancy in California. I have always maintained that a perfect system might be invented, by which the game of poker may be made to yield a certain percentage to the intelligent player. I am not at liberty at present to disclose the system ; but before leaving this city I intend to perfect it." He seems to have done so, and returned to Monte Flat with two dollars and thirty-seven cents, the absolute remainder of his capital after such perfection.

It was not until 1868 that he appeared to have finally succeeded in going home. He left us by the overland route—a route which he declared would give great opportunity for the discovery of undeveloped resources. His last letter was dated Virginia City. He was absent three years. At the close of a very hot day in midsummer he alighted from the Wingdam stage, with hair and beard powdered with dust and age. There was a certain shyness about his greeting, quite different from his frank volubility, that did not, however, impress us as any accession of character. For some days he was reserved regarding his recent visit, contenting himself with asserting, with more or less aggressiveness, that he had "always said he was going home, and now he had been there." Later he grew more communicative, and spoke freely and critically of the manners and customs of New York and Boston, commented on the social changes in the years of his absence, and, I remember, was very hard upon what he deemed the follies incidental to a high state of civilization. Still later he darkly alluded to the moral laxity of the higher planes of Eastern society; but it was not long before he completely tore away the veil, and revealed the naked wickedness of New York social life in a way I even now shudder to recall. Vinous intoxication, it appeared, was a common habit of the first ladies of the city. Immoralities which he scarcely dared name were daily practised by the refined of both sexes. Niggardliness and greed were the common vices of the rich. "I have always asserted," he continued, "that corruption must exist where luxury and riches are rampant, and capital is not used to develop the natural resources of the country. Thank you—I will take mine without sugar." It is possible that some of these painful details crept into the local journals. I remember an editorial in the *Monte Flat Monitor*, entitled "The Effete East," in which the fatal decadence of New York and New England was elaborately stated, and California offered as a means of natural salvation. " Perhaps," said the *Monitor*, "we might add that Calaveras County offers superior inducements to the Eastern visitor with capital."

Later he spoke of his family. The daughter he had left a child had grown into beautiful woman-hood. The son was already taller and larger than his father ; and, in a playful trial of strength, " the young rascal," added Plunkett, with a voice broken with paternal pride and humorous objurgation, had twice thrown his doting parent to the ground. But it was of his daughter he chiefly spoke. Perhaps emboldened by the evident interest which masculine Monte Flat held in feminine beauty, he expatiated at some length on her various charms and accomplishments, and finally produced her photograph—that of a very pretty girl—to their infinite peril. But his account of his first meeting with her was so peculiar, that I must fain give it after his own methods, which were, perhaps, some shades less precise and elegant than his written style.

"You see, boys, it's always been my opinion that a man oughter be able to tell his own flesh and blood by instinct. It's ten years since I'd seen my Melindy ; and she was then only seven, and about so high. So when I went to New York, what did I do ? Did I go straight to my house, and ask for my wife and daughter, like other folks ? No, sir ! I rigged myself up as a pedlar, as a

pedlar, sir; and I rung the bell. When the
servant came to the door, I wanted—don't you
see?—to show the ladies some trinkets. Then
there was a voice over the banisters says, ' Don't
want anything: send him away.'—' Some nice
laces, ma'am, smuggled,' I says, looking up.
'Get out, you wretch!' says she. I knew the
voice, boys: it was my wife, sure as a gun. Thar
wasn't any instinct thar. 'Maybe the young ladies
want somethin',' I said. ' Did you hear me?' says
she; and with that she jumps forward, and I left.
It's ten years, boys, since I've seen the old woman;
but somehow, when she fetched that leap, I naterally left."

He had been standing beside the bar—his usual
attitude—when he made this speech; but at this
point he half faced his auditors with a look that
was very effective. Indeed, a few who had ex-
hibited some signs of scepticism and lack of interest, at once assumed an appearance of intense
gratification and curiosity as he went on.

"Well, by hangin' round there for a day or two,
I found out at last it was to be Melindy's birthday
next week, and that she was goin' to have a big
party. I tell ye what, boys, it weren't no slouch
of a reception. The whole house was bloomin'
with flowers, and blazin' with lights; and there
was no end of servants, and plate, and refreshments,
and fixin's—— "

"Uncle Joe."

" Well ? "

" Where did they get the money ? "

Plunkett faced his interlocutor with a severe glance. " I always said," he replied slowly, " that, when I went home, I'd send on ahead of me a draft for ten thousand dollars. I always said that, didn't I ? Eh ? And I said I was goin' home— and I've been home, haven't I ? Well ? "

Either there was something irresistibly conclusive in this logic, or else the desire to hear the remainder of Plunkett s story was stronger ; but there were no more interruptions. His ready good-humour quickly returned, and, with a slight chuckle, he went on,—

" I went to the biggest jewelry shop in town, and I bought a pair of diamond ear-rings, and put them in my pocket, and went to the house. ' What name ? ' says the chap who opened the door ; and he looked like a cross 'twixt a restaurant waiter and a parson. ' Skeesicks,' said I. He takes me in ; and pretty soon my wife comes sailin' into the parlour and says, ' Excuse me ; but I don't think I recognise the name.' She was mighty polite ; for I had on a red wig and side-whiskers. ' A friend of your husband's from California, ma'am, with a present for your daughter, Miss——,' and I made as I had forgot the name. But all of a sudden a voice said, ' That's too thin ; ' and in walked Melindy. ' It's playin' it rather low down, father, to pretend you don't know your daughter's name ;

ain't it now? How are you, old man?' And with that she tears off my wig and whiskers, and throws her arms round my neck—instinct, sir, pure instinct!"

Emboldened by the laughter which followed his description of the filial utterances of Melinda, he again repeated her speech, with more or less elaboration, joining in with, and indeed often leading, the hilarity that accompanied it, and returning to it, with more or less incoherency, several times during the evening.

And so, at various times and at various places, but chiefly in bar-rooms, did this Ulysses of Monte Flat recount the story of his wanderings. There were several discrepancies in his statement; there was sometimes considerable prolixity of detail; there was occasional change of character and scenery; there was once or twice an absolute change in the *dénouement :* but always the fact of his having visited his wife and children remained. Of course, in a sceptical community like that of Monte Flat—a community accustomed to great expectation and small realization—a community wherein, to use the local dialect, "they got the colour, and struck hardpan," more frequently than any other mining camp—in such a community the fullest credence was not given to old man Plunkett's facts. There was only one exception to the general unbelief—Henry York, of Sandy Bar. It was he who was always an attentive listener; it was his scant purse that had often furnished

Plunkett with means to pursue his unprofitable speculations ; it was to him that the charms of Melinda were more frequently rehearsed; it was he that had borrowed her photograph ; and it was he that, sitting alone in his little cabin one night, kissed that photograph, until his honest, handsome face glowed again in the firelight.

It was dusty in Monte Flat. The ruins of the long dry season were crumbling everywhere : everywhere the dying summer had strewn its red ashes a foot deep, or exhaled its last breath in a red cloud above the troubled highways. The alders and cottonwoods, that marked the line of the watercourses, were grimy with dust, and looked as if they might have taken root in the open air. The gleaming stones of the parched watercourses themselves were as dry bones in the valley of death. The dusty sunset at times painted the flanks of the distant hills a dull coppery hue : on other days, there was an odd, indefinable earthquake halo on the volcanic cones of the farther coast-spurs. Again an acrid, resinous smoke from the burning wood on Heavytree Hill smarted the eyes, and choked the free breath of Monte Flat ; or a fierce wind, driving everything, including the shrivelled summer, like a curled leaf before it, swept down the flanks of the Sierras, and chased the inhabitants to the doors of their cabins, and shook its red fist in at their windows. And on such a night as this, the dust having in some way choked the

wheels of material progress in Monte Flat, most of
the inhabitants were gathered listlessly in the
gilded bar-room of the Moquelumne Hotel, spitting
silently at the red-hot stove that tempered the
mountain winds to the shorn lambs of Monte Flat,
and waiting for the rain.

Every method known to the Flat of beguiling
the time until the advent of this long-looked-for
phenomenon had been tried. It is true the
methods were not many, being limited chiefly to
that form of popular facetiæ known as practical
joking; and even this had assumed the seriousness of a business pursuit. Tommy Roy, who had
spent two hours in digging a ditch in front of his
own door, into which a few friends casually dropped
during the evening, looked *ennuyé* and dissatisfied.
The four prominent citizens, who, disguised as foot-
pads, had stopped the county treasurer on the
Wingdam road, were jaded from their playful
efforts next morning. The principal physician and
lawyer of Monte Flat, who had entered into an
unhallowed conspiracy to compel the sheriff of
Calaveras and his *posse* to serve a writ of ejectment
on a grizzly bear, feebly disguised under the name
of one "Major Ursus," who haunted the groves of
Heavytree Hill, wore an expression of resigned
weariness. Even the editor of the *Monte Flat
Monitor*, who had that morning written a glowing
account of a battle with the Whipneck Indians, for
the benefit of Eastern readers—even *he* looked

grave and worn. When at last Abner Dean of Angel's, who had been on a visit to San Francisco, walked into the room, he was, of course, victimized in the usual way by one or two apparently honest questions, which ended in his answering them, and then falling into the trap of asking another, to his utter and complete shame and mortification ; but that was all. Nobody laughed ; and Abner, although a victim, did not lose his good-humour. He turned quietly on his tormentors, and said—

"I've got something better than that—you know old man Plunkett ? "

Everybody simultaneously spat at the stove, and nodded his head.

"You know he went home three years ago ? "

Two or three changed the position of their legs from the backs of different chairs ; and one man said, "Yes."

" Had a good time, home ? "

Everybody looked cautiously at the man who had said "Yes ; " and he, accepting the responsibility with a faint-hearted smile, said " Yes " again, and breathed hard. " Saw his wife and child—purty gal ? " said Abner, cautiously. " Yes," answered the man, doggedly. " Saw her photograph, perhaps ? " continued Abner Dean, quietly.

The man looked hopelessly around for support. Two or three who had been sitting near him, and evidently encouraging him with a look of interest, now shamelessly abandoned him, and looked another way. Henry York flushed a little, and veiled his grey eyes. The man hesitated, and then with a sickly smile, that was intended to convey the fact that he was perfectly aware of the object of this questioning, and was only humouring it from abstract good feeling, returned "Yes," again.

"Sent home—let's see—ten thousand dollars, wasn't it?" Abner Dean went on. "Yes" reiterated the man, with the same smile.

"Well, I thought so," said Abner, quietly. "But the fact is, you see, that he never went home at all—nary time."

Everybody stared at Abner in genuine surprise and interest, as, with provoking calmness and a half-lazy manner, he went on—

"You see, thar was a man down in 'Frisco as knowed him, and saw him in Sonora during the whole of that three years. He was herding sheep, or tending cattle, or spekilating, all that time, and hadn't a red cent. Well, it 'mounts to this,—that 'ar Plunkett ain't been east of the Rocky Mountains since '49."

The laugh which Abner Dean had the right to confidently expect came; but it was bitter and sardonic. I think indignation was apparent in the minds of his hearers. It was felt, for the first time, that there was a limit to practical joking. A deception carried on for a year, compromising the sagacity of Monte Flat, was deserving the severest reprobation. Of course, nobody had

believed Plunkett ; but then the supposition that
it might be believed in adjacent camps that they
had believed him was gall and bitterness. The
lawyer thought that an indictment for obtaining
money under false pretences might be found. The
physician had long suspected him of insanity, and
was not certain but that he ought to be confined.
The four prominent merchants thought that the
business interests of Monte Flat demanded that
something should be done. In the midst of an
excited and angry discussion, the door slowly
opened, and old man Plunkett staggered into the
room.

He had changed pitifully in the last six months.
His hair was a dusty, yellowish grey, like the
chemisal on the flanks of Heavytree Hill ; his face
was waxen white, and blue and puffy under the
eyes ; his clothes were soiled and shabby, streaked
in front with the stains of hurriedly-eaten lunch-
eons, and fluffy behind with the wool and hair
of hurriedly-extemporized couches. In obedience
to that odd law, that the more seedy and soiled a
man's garments become, the less does he seem
inclined to part with them, even during that
portion of the twenty-four hours when they are
deemed less essential, Plunkett's clothes had gradually taken on the appearance of a kind of a
bark, or an outgrowth from within, for which their
possessor was not entirely responsible. Howbeit,
as he entered the room, he attempted to button

his coat over a dirty shirt, and passed his fingers, after the manner of some animal, over his cracker-strewn beard, in recognition of a cleanly public sentiment. But, even as he did so, the weak smile faded from his lips; and his hand, after fumbling aimlessly around a button, dropped helplessly at his side. For as he leaned his back against the bar, and faced the group, he, for the first time, became aware that every eye but one was fixed upon him. His quick, nervous apprehension at once leaped to the truth. His miserable secret was out, and abroad in the very air about him. As a last resort, he glanced despairingly at Henry York; but his flushed face was turned towards the windows.

No word was spoken. As the bar-keeper silently swung a decanter and glass before him, he took a cracker from a dish, and mumbled it with affected unconcern. He lingered over his liquor until its potency stiffened his relaxed sinews, and dulled the nervous edge of his apprehension, and then he suddenly faced around. "It don't look as if we were going to hev any rain much afore Christmas," he said, with defiant ease.

No one made any reply.

"Just like this in '52, and again in '60. It's always been my opinion that these dry seasons come reg'lar. I've said it afore. I say it again. It's jist as I said about going home, you know," he added, with desperate recklessness.

"Thar's a man," said Abner Dean, lazily, "ez sez you never went home. Thar's a man ez sez you've been three years in Sonora. Thar's a man ez sez you hain't seen your wife and daughter since '49. Thar's a man ez sez you've been playin' this camp for six months."

There was a dead silence. Then a voice said quite as quietly—

"That man lies."

It was not the old man's voice. Everybody turned as Henry York slowly rose, stretching out his six feet of length, and, brushing away the ashes that had fallen from his pipe upon his breast, deliberately placed himself beside Plunkett, and faced the others.

"That man ain't here," continued Abner Dean, with listless indifference of voice, and a gentle preoccupation of manner, as he carelessly allowed his right hand to rest on his hip near his revolver. "That man ain't here ; but, if I'm called upon to make good what he says, why I'm on hand."

All rose as the two men—perhaps the least externally agitated of them all—approached each other. The lawyer stepped in between them.

"Perhaps there's some mistake here. York, do you *know* that the old man has been home ?"

"Yes."

"How do you know it ?"

York turned his clear, honest, frank eyes on his questioner, and without a tremour told the only

I

direct and unmitigated lie of his life. " Because I've seen him there."

The answer was conclusive. It was known that York had been visiting the East during the old man's absence. The colloquy had diverted attention from Plunkett, who, pale and breathless, was staring at his unexpected deliverer. As he turned again towards his tormentors, there was something in the expression of his eye that caused those that were nearest to him to fall back, and sent a strange, indefinable thrill through the boldest and most reckless. As he made a step forward, the physician, almost unconsciously, raised his hand with a warning gesture; and old man Plunkett, with his eyes fixed upon the red-hot stove, and an odd smile playing about his mouth, began—

" Yes—of course you did. Who says you didn't? It ain't no lie. I said I was goin' home—and I've been home. Haven't I? My God! I have. Who says I've been lyin'? Who says I'm dreamin'? Is it true—why don't you speak? It is true, after all. You say you saw me there: why don't you speak again? Say, say!—is it true? It's going now. O my God! it's going again. It's going now. Save me!" And with a fierce cry he fell forward in a fit upon the floor.

When the old man regained his senses, he found himself in York's cabin. A flickering fire of pine-boughs lit up the rude rafters, and fell upon a photograph tastefully framed with fir-cones, and hung above the brush whereon he lay. It was the portrait of a young girl. It was the first object to meet the old man's gaze ; and it brought with it a flush of such painful consciousness, that he started, and glanced quickly around. But his eyes only encountered those of York—clear, grey, critical, and patient—and they fell again.

"Tell me, old man," said York, not unkindly but with the same cold, clear tone in his voice that his eye betrayed a moment ago—"tell me, is *that* a lie too?" and he pointed to the picture.

The old man closed his eyes, and did not reply. Two hours before, the question would have stung him into some evasion or bravado. But the revelation contained in the question, as well as the tone of York's voice, was to him now, in his pitiable condition, a relief. It was plain, even to his confused brain, that York had lied when he had indorsed his story in the bar-room ; it was clear to him now that he had not been home, that he was not, as he had begun to fear, going mad. It was such a relief, that, with characteristic weakness, his former recklessness and extravagance returned. He began to chuckle, finally to laugh uproariously.

York, with his eyes still fixed on the old man, withdrew the hand with which he had taken his.

"Didn't we fool 'em nicely : eh, Yorky! He, he! The biggest thing yet ever played in this camp! I always said I'd play 'em all some day, I have—played 'em for six months. Ain't it rich

—ain't it the richest thing you ever seed? Did you
see Abner's face when he spoke 'bout that man as
seed me in Sonora? Warn't it good as the min-
strels? Oh, it's too much!" and, striking his leg
with the palm of his hand, he almost threw himself
from the bed in a paroxysm of laughter—a paroxysm that, nevertheless, appeared to be half real
and half affected.

"Is that photograph hers?" said York, in a low
voice, after a slight pause.

"Hers? No! It's one of the San Francisco
actresses. He, he! Don't you see? I bought it
for two bits in one of the bookstores. I never
thought they'd swaller *that* too; but they did!
Oh, but the old man played 'em this time didn't
he—eh?" and he peered curiously in York's face.

"Yes, and he played *me* too," said York, looking
steadily in the old man's eye.

"Yes, of course," interposed Plunkett hastily;
"but you know, Yorky, you got out of it well!
You've sold 'em too. We've both got 'm on a
string now—you and me—got to stick together
now. You did it well, Yorky: you did it well.
Why, when you said you'd seen me in York City,
I'm d—d if I didn't——"

"Didn't what?" said York, gently; for the old
man had stopped with a pale face and wandering eye.

"Eh?"

"You say when I said I had seen you in New
York you thought ——"

"You lie! said the old man, fiercely. "I didn't say I thought anything. What are you trying to go back on me for, eh?" His hands were trembling as he rose muttering from the bed, and made his way towards the hearth.

"Gimme some whiskey," he said presently, "and dry up. You oughter treat anyway. Them fellows oughter treated last night. By hookey, I'd made 'em—only I fell sick."

York placed the liquor and a tin cup on the table beside him, and, going to the door, turned his back upon his guest, and looked out on the night. Although it was clear moonlight, the familiar prospect never to him seemed so dreary. The dead waste of the broad Wingdam highway never seemed so monotonous, so like the days that he had passed, and were to come to him, so like the old man in its suggestion of going some time, and never getting there. He turned, and going up to Plunkett, put his hand upon his shoulder, and said—

"I want you to answer one question fairly and squarely."

The liquor seemed to have warmed the torpid blood in the old man's veins, and softened his acerbity ; for the face he turned up to York was mellowed in its rugged outline, and more thoughtful in expression, as he said—

"Go on, my boy."

"Have you a wife and—daughter?"

" Before God I have ! "

The two men were silent for a moment, both gazing at the fire. Then Plunkett began rubbing his knees slowly.

" The wife, if it comes to that, ain't much," he began cautiously, " being a little on the shoulder, you know, and wantin', so to speak, a liberal California education, which makes, you know, a bad combination. It's always been my opinion, that there ain't any worse. Why, she's as ready with her tongue as Abner Dean is with his revolver, only with the difference that she shoots from principle, as she calls it ; and the consequence is, she's always layin' for you. It's the effete East, my boy, that's ruinin' her. It's them ideas she gets in New York and Boston that's made her and me what we are. I don't mind her havin' 'em, if she didn't shoot. But, havin' that propensity, them principles oughtn't to be lying round loose no more'n firearms."

" But your daughter ? " said York.

The old man's hands went up to his eyes here, and then both hands and head dropped forward on the table. " Don't say anything 'bout her, my boy, don't ask me now." With one hand concealing his eyes, he fumbled about with the other in his pockets for his handkerchief—but vainly. Perhaps it was owing to this fact, that he repressed his tears ; for, when he removed his hand from his eyes, they were quite dry. Then he found his voice.

"She's a beautiful girl, beautiful, though I say it; and you shall see her, my boy—you shall see her sure. I've got things about fixed now. I shall have my plan for reducin' ores perfected in a day or two ; and I've got proposals from all the smeltin' works here" (here he hastily produced a bundle of papers that fell upon the floor), "and I'm goin' to send for em. I've got the papers here as will give me ten thousand dollars clear in the next month," he added, as he strove to collect the valuable documents again. " I'll have 'em here by Christmas, if I live ; and you shall eat your Christmas dinner with me, York, my boy—you shall sure."

With his tongue now fairly loosened by liquor and the suggestive vastness of his prospects, he rambled on more or less incoherently, elaborating and amplifying his plans, occasionally even speaking of them as already accomplished, until the moon rode high in the heavens, and York led him again to his couch. Here he lay for some time muttering to himself, until at last he sank into a heavy sleep. When York had satisfied himself of the fact, he gently took down the picture and frame, and, going to the hearth, tossed them on the dying embers, and sat down to see them burn.

The fir-cones leaped instantly into flame ; then the features that had entranced San Francisco audiences nightly, flashed up and passed away (as such things are apt to pass) ; and even the cynical smile on York's lips faded too. And then there came a supplemental and unexpected flash as the embers fell together, and by its light York saw a paper upon the floor. It was one that had fallen from the old man's pocket. As he picked it up list-lessly, a photograph slipped from its folds. It was the portrait of a young girl; and on its reverse was written in a scrawling hand, "Melinda to father."

It was at best a cheap picture, but, ah me! I fear even the deft graciousness of the highest art could not have softened the rigid angularities of that youthful figure, its self-complacent vulgarity, its cheap finery, its expressionless ill-favour. York did not look at it a second time. He turned to the letter for relief.

It was misspelled; it was unpunctuated; it was almost illegible; it was fretful in tone, and selfish in sentiment. It was not, I fear, even original in the story of its woes. It was the harsh recital of poverty, of suspicion, of mean makeshifts and com-promises, of low pains and lower longings, of sor-rows that were degrading, of a grief that was piti-able. Yet it was sincere in a certain kind of vague yearning for the presence of the degraded man to whom it was written—an affection that was more like a confused instinct than a sentiment.

York folded it again carefully, and placed it beneath the old man's pillow. Then he returned to his seat by the fire. A smile that had been playing upon his face, deepening the curves behind his moustache, and gradually overrunning his clear grey eyes, presently faded away. It was last to go from his eyes; and it left there, oddly enough to those who did not know him, a tear.

He sat there for a long time, leaning forward, his head upon his hands. The wind that had been striving with the canvas roof all at once lifted its edges, and a moonbeam slipped suddenly in, and lay for a moment like a shining blade upon his shoulder; and, knighted by its touch, straightway plain Henry York arose, sustained, high-purposed, and self-reliant.

The rains had come at last. There was already a visible greenness on the slopes of Heavytree Hill; and the long, white track of the Wingdam road was lost in outlying pools and ponds a hundred rods from Monte Flat. The spent water-courses, whose white bones had been sinuously trailed over the flat, like the vertebræ of some forgotten saurian, were full again; the dry bones moved once more in the valley; and there was joy in the ditches, and a pardonable extravagance in the columns of the *Monte Flat Monitor.* "Never before in the history of the county has the yield been so satisfactory. Our contemporary of the *Hillside Beacon,* who yesterday facetiously alluded to the fact (?) that our best citizens were leaving town in 'dugouts,' on account of the flood, will be glad to hear that our distinguished fellow-townsman, Mr: Henry York, now on a visit to his relatives in the East, lately took with him in his 'dugout' the modest sum of fifty thousand dollars, the result of one week's clean up. We can imagine," continued that sprightly journal, " that no such misfortune is likely to overtake Hillside this season. And yet we believe the *Beacon* man wants a railroad." A few journals broke out into poetry. The operator at Simpson's Crossing telegraphed to the *Sacramento Universe:* " All day the low clouds have shook their garnered fulness down." A San Francisco journal lapsed into noble verse, thinly disguised as editorial prose : " Rejoice : the gentle rain has come, the bright and pearly rain, which scatters blessings on the hills, and sifts them o'er the plain. Rejoice," &c. Indeed, there was only one to whom the rain had not brought blessing, and that was Plunkett. In some mysterious and darksome way, it had interfered with the perfection of his new method of reducing ores, and thrown the advent of that invention back another season. It had brought him down to an habitual seat in the bar-room, where, to heedless and inattentive ears, he sat and discoursed of the East and his family.

No one disturbed him. Indeed, it was rumoured that some funds had been lodged with the landlord, by a person or persons unknown, whereby his few wants were provided for. His mania—for that was the charitable construction which Monte Flat put upon his conduct—was indulged, even to the

extent of Monte Flat's accepting his invitation to
dine with his family on Christmas Day—an invitation extended frankly to everyone with whom
the old man drank or talked. But one day, to
everybody's astonishment, he burst into the bar-
room, holding an open letter in his hand. It read
as follows :—

"Be ready to meet your family at the new cottage on the
Heavytree Hill on Christmas Day. Invite what friends you
choose.

"HENRY YORK."

The letter was handed round in silence. The
old man, with a look alternating between hope and
fear, gazed in the faces of the group. The doctor,
looked up significantly, after a pause. "It's a
forgery evidently," he said in a low voice. "He's
cunning enough to conceive it (they always are) ;
but you'll find he'll fail in executing it. Watch
his face !—Old man," he said suddenly, in a loud
peremptory tone, "this is a trick, a forgery, and
you know it. Answer me squarely, and look me
in the eye. Isn't it so ? "

The eyes of Plunkett stared a moment, and
then dropped weakly. Then, with a feebler smile,
he said, "You're too many for me, boys. The
Doc's right. The little game's up. You can take
the old man's hat ; " and so, tottering, trembling,
and chuckling, he dropped into silence and his
accustomed seat. But the next day he seemed to

have forgotten this episode, and talked as glibly as ever of the approaching festivity.

And so the days and weeks passed until Christmas—a bright, clear day, warmed with south winds, and joyous with the resurrection of springing grasses—broke upon Monte Flat. And then there was a sudden commotion in the hotel bar-room ; and Abner Dean stood beside the old man's chair, and shook him out of a slumber to his feet. "Rouse up, old man. York is here, with your wife and daughter, at the cottage on Heavytree. Come, old man. Here, boys, give him a lift ; " and in another moment a dozen strong and willing hands had raised the old man, and bore him in triumph to the street, up the steep grade of Heavy-tree Hill, and deposited him, struggling and confused, in the porch of a little cottage. At the same instant two women rushed forward, but were restrained by a gesture from Henry York. The old man was struggling to his feet. With an effort at last, he stood erect, trembling, his eye fixed, a grey pallor on his cheek, and a deep resonance in his voice.

"It's all a trick, and a lie ! They ain't no flesh and blood or kin o' mine. It ain't my wife, nor child. My daughter's a beautiful girl—a beautiful girl, d'ye hear ? She's in New York with her mother, and I'm going to fetch her here. I said I'd go home, and I've been home : d'ye hear me ? I've been home ! It's a mean trick you're playin' on the old man. Let me go : d'ye hear? Keep them women off me ! Let me go ! I'm going—I'm going —home !"

His hands were thrown up convulsively in the air, and, half turning round, he fell sideways on the porch, and so to the ground. They picked him up hurriedly, but too late. He had gone home.

I T was at a little mining-camp in the California Sierras that he first dawned upon me in all his grotesque sweetness.

I had arrived early in the morning, but not in time to intercept the friend who was the object of my visit. He had gone " prospecting"—so they told me on the river—and would not probably return until late in the afternoon. They could not say what direction he had taken ; they could not suggest that I would be likely to find him if I followed. But it was the general opinion that I had better wait.

I looked around me. I was standing upon the bank of the river ; and apparently the only other human beings in the world were my interlocutors, who were even then just disappearing from my horizon, down the steep bank, towards the river's dry bed. I approached the edge of the bank.

Where could I wait ?

Oh ! anywhere—down with them on the river-bar, where they were working, if I liked. Or I could make myself at home in any of those cabins that I found lying round loose. Or perhaps it would be cooler and pleasanter for me in my

friend's cabin on the hill. Did I see those three
large sugar-pines, and, a little to the right, a canvas
roof and chimney, over the bushes? Well, that
was my friend's—that was Dick Sylvester's cabin.
I could stake my horse in that little hollow, and
just hang round there till he came. I would find
some books in the shanty. I could amuse myself
with them ; or I could play with the baby.

Do what ?

But they had already gone. I leaned over the
bank, and called after their vanishing figures—

"What did you say I could do?"

The answer floated slowly up on the hot, sluggish
air—

"Pla-a-y with the baby."

The lazy echoes took it up, and tossed it languidly from hill to hill, until Bald Mountain
opposite made some incoherent remark about the
baby ; and then all was still.

I must have been mistaken. My friend was not
a man of family ; there was not a woman within
forty miles of the river camp ; he never was so
passionately devoted to children as to import a
luxury so expensive. I must have been mistaken.

I turned my horse's head towards the hill. As
we slowly climbed the narrow trail, the little settlement might have been some exhumed Pompeian
suburb, so deserted and silent were its habitations.
The open doors plainly disclosed each rudely-fur-
nished interior—the rough pine table, with the

scant equipage of the morning meal still standing ;
the wooden bunk, with its tumbled and dishevelled
blankets. A golden lizard, the very genius of
desolate stillness, had stopped breathless upon the
threshold of one cabin ; a squirrel peeped impu-
dently into the window of another ; a woodpecker,
with the general flavour of undertaking which dis-
tinguishes that bird, withheld his sepulchral ham-
mer from the coffin-lid of the roof on which he
was professionally engaged, as we passed. For a
moment I half regretted that I had not accepted
the invitation to the river-bed ; but, the next
moment, a breeze swept up the long, dark cañon,
and the waiting files of the pines beyond bent
towards me in salutation. I think my horse understood, as well as myself, that it was the cabins that
made the solitude human, and therefore unbear-
able ; for he quickened his pace, and with a gentle
trot brought me to the edge of the wood, and the
three pines that stood like videttes before the
Sylvester outpost.

Unsaddling my horse in the little hollow, I
unslung the long *riata* from the saddle-bow, and,
tethering him to a young sapling, turned towards
the cabin. But I had gone only a few steps, when
I heard a quick trot behind me ; and poor Pomposo, with every fibre tingling with fear, was at my
heels. I looked hurriedly around. The breeze
had died away ; and only an occasional breath
from the deep-chested woods, more like a long

sigh than any articulate sound, or the dry singing
of a cicala in the heated cañon, were to be heard;
I examined the ground carefully for rattlesnakes,
but in vain. Yet here was Pomposo shivering
from his arched neck to his sensitive haunches, his
very flanks pulsating with terror. I soothed him
as well as I could, and then walked to the edge of
the wood, and peered into its dark recesses. The
bright flash of a bird's wing, or the quick dart of a
squirrel, was all I saw. I confess it was with something of superstitious expectation that I again
turned towards the cabin. A fairy child, attended
by Titania and her train, lying in an expensive
cradle, would not have surprised me : a Sleeping
Beauty, whose awakening would have repeopled
these solitudes with life and energy, I am afraid I
began confidently to look for, and would have
kissed without hesitation.

But I found none of these. Here was the
evidence of my friend's taste and refinement, in the
hearth swept scrupulously clean, in the picturesque
arrangement of the fur-skins that covered the floor
and furniture, and the striped *serápe** lying on the
wooden couch. Here were the walls fancifully
papered with illustrations from the *London News ;*
here was the woodcut portrait of Mr. Emerson
over the chimney, quaintly framed with blue-jays'
wings ; here were his few favourite books on the

* A fine Mexican blanket, used as an outer garment for
riding.

swinging shelf; and here, lying upon the couch, the latest copy of *Punch*. Dear Dick! The flour-sack was sometimes empty; but the gentle satirist seldom missed his weekly visit.

I threw myself on the couch, and tried to read. But I soon exhausted my interest in my friend's library, and lay there staring through the open door on the green hillside beyond. The breeze again sprang up; and a delicious coolness, mixed with the rare incense of the woods, stole through the cabin. The slumbrous droning of bumblebees outside the canvas roof, the faint cawing of rooks on the opposite mountain, and the fatigue of my morning ride, began to droop my eyelids. I pulled the *scrápe* over me, as a precaution against the freshening mountain breeze, and in a few moments was asleep.

I do not remember how long I slept. I must have been conscious, however, during my slumber, of my inability to keep myself covered by the *scrápe;* for I awoke once or twice, clutching it with a despairing hand as it was disappearing over the foot of the couch. Then I became suddenly aroused to the fact that my efforts to retain it were resisted by some equally persistent force; and, letting it go, I was horrified at seeing it swiftly drawn under the couch. At this point I sat up completely awake; for immediately after, what seemed to be an exaggerated muff began to emerge from under the couch. Presently it appeared fully, dragging the *scrápe* after it. There was no mis-

taking it now : it was a baby-bear—a mere suck-
ling, it was true, a helpless roll of fat and fur, but
unmistakably a grizzly cub.

I cannot recall anything more irresistibly ludi-
crous than its aspect as it slowly raised its small,
wondering eyes to mine. It was so much taller on
its haunches than its shoulders, its forelegs were
so disproportionately small, that, in walking, its
hind feet invariably took precedence. It was per-
petually pitching forward over its pointed, inoffen-
sive nose, and recovering itself always, after these
involuntary somersaults, with the gravest astonishment. To add to its preposterous appearance, one
of its hind feet was adorned by a shoe of Sylvester's, into which it had accidentally and inex-
tricably stepped. As this somewhat impeded its
first impulse to fly, it turned to me ; and then,
possibly recognizing in the stranger the same spe-
cies as its master, it paused. Presently it slowly
raised itself on its hind-legs, and vaguely and
deprecatingly waved a baby-paw, fringed with
little hooks of steel. I took the paw, and shook it
gravely. From that moment we were friends.
The little affair of the *serápe* was forgotten.

Nevertheless, I was wise enough to cement our
friendship by an act of delicate courtesy. Following the direction of his eyes, I had no difficulty in
finding on a shelf near the ridge-pole the sugar-
box and the square lumps of white sugar that even
the poorest miner is never without. While he was

eating them, I had time to examine him more
closely. His body was a silky, dark, but exquisitely-
modulated grey, deepening to black in his paws
and muzzle. His fur was excessively long, thick, and
soft as eider-down; the cushions of flesh beneath
perfectly infantine in their texture and contour.
He was so very young, that the palms of his half-
human feet were still tender as a baby's.   Except
for the bright blue, steely hooks, half-sheathed in
his little toes, there was not a single harsh outline
or detail in his plump figure.   He was as free from
angles as one of Leda's offspring.   Your caressing
hand sank away in his fur with dreamy langour.
To look at him long was an intoxication of the
senses; to pat him was a wild delirium; to embrace him, an utter demoralization of the intel-
lectual faculties.

When he had finished the sugar, he rolled out of
the door with a half-diffident, half-inviting look in
his eyes as if he expected me to follow.   I did so;
but the sniffing and snorting of the keen-scented
Pomposo in the hollow not only revealed the cause
of his former terror, but decided me to take
another direction.   After a moment's hesitation, he
concluded to go with me, although I am satisfied,
from a certain impish look in his eye, that he fully
understood and rather enjoyed the fright of Pomposo.   As he rolled along at my side, with a gait
not unlike a drunken sailor, I discovered that his
long hair concealed a leather collar around his

neck, which bore for its legend the single word
" Baby ! " I recalled the mysterious suggestion of
the two miners. This, then, was the "baby" with
whom I was to "play."

How we "played ; " how Baby allowed me to roll
him down hill, crawling and puffing up again each
time with perfect good humour ; how he climbed
a young sapling after my Panama hat, which
I had "shied" into one of the topmost branches ;
how, after getting it, he refused to descend until it
suited his pleasure ; how, when he did come down,
he persisted in walking about on three legs, carrying my hat, a crushed and shapeless mass, clasped
to his breast with the remaining one : how I missed
him at last, and finally discovered him seated on a
table in one of the tenantless cabins, with a bottle
of syrup between his paws, vainly endeavouring to
extract its contents—these and other details of
that eventful day I shall not weary the reader with
now. Enough that, when Dick Sylvester returned,
I was pretty well fagged out, and the baby was
rolled up, an immense bolster, at the foot of the
couch, asleep. Sylvester's first words after our
greeting were—

" Isn't he delicious ? "

" Perfectly. Where did you get him ? "

" Lying under his dead mother, five miles from
here," said Dick, lighting his pipe. " Knocked her
over at fifty yards : perfectly clean shot ; never
moved afterwards. Baby crawled out, scared, but

unhurt. She must have been carrying him in her mouth, and dropped him when she faced me; for he wasn't more than three days old, and not steady on his pins. He takes the only milk that comes to the settlement, brought up by Adams' Express at seven o'clock every morning. They say he looks like me. Do you think so?" asked Dick with perfect gravity, stroking his hay-coloured mustachios, and evidently assuming his best expression.

I took leave of the baby early the next morning in Sylvester's cabin, and, out of respect to Pomposo's feelings, rode by without any postscript of expression. But the night before I had made Sylvester solemnly swear, that, in the event of any separation between himself and Baby, it should revert to me. "At the same time," he had added, "it's only fair to say that I don't think of dying just yet, old fellow; and I don't know of anything else that would part the cub and me."

Two months after this conversation, as I was turning over the morning's mail at my office in San Francisco, I noticed a letter bearing Sylvester's familiar hand. But it was post-marked "Stockton," and I opened it with some anxiety at once. Its contents were as follows :

"O FRANK!—Don't you remember what we agreed upon anent the baby? Well, consider me as dead for the next six months, or gone where cubs can't follow me—East. I know you love the baby; but do you think, dear boy—now,

really, do you think you *could* be a father to it? Consider
this well. You are young, thoughtless, well-meaning enough ;
but dare you take upon yourself the functions of guide,
genius, or guardian to one so young and guileless? Could
you be the Mentor to this Telemachus? Think of the
temptations of a metropolis. Look at the question well,
and let me know speedily ; for I've got him as far as this
place, and he's kicking up an awful row in the hotel yard.
and rattling his chain like a maniac. Let me know by tele-
graph at once.

" SYLVESTER.

" P.S.—Of course he's grown a little, and doesn't take
things always as quietly as he did. He dropped rather
heavily on two of Watson's 'purps' last week, and snatched
old Watson himself bald headed, for interfering. You remember Watson? For an intelligent man, he knows very
little of California fauna. How are you fixed for bears on
Montgomery Street, I mean in regard to corrals and things ?

" P.P.S.—He's got some new tricks. The boys have been
teaching him to put up his hands with them. He slings an
ugly left. " S. "

I am afraid that my desire to possess myself of
Baby overcame all other considerations ; and I
telegraphed an affirmative at once to Sylvester.
When I reached my lodgings late that afternoon,
my landlady was awaiting me with a telegram. It
was two lines from Sylvester—

"All right. Baby goes down on night-boat. Be a father
to him. " S. "

It was due, then, at one o'clock that night. For
a moment I was staggered at my own precipitation.
I had as yet made no preparations, had said nothing to my landlady about her new guest. I

expected to arrange everything in time ; and now, through Sylvester's indecent haste, that time had been shortened twelve hours.

Something, however, must be done at once. I turned to Mrs. Brown. I had great reliance in her maternal instincts : I had that still greater reliance common to our sex in the general tender-heartedness of pretty women. But I confess I was alarmed. Yet, with a feeble smile, I tried to introduce the subject with classical ease and light-ness. I even said, "If Shakspeare's Athenian clown, Mrs. Brown, believed that a lion among ladies was a dreadful thing, what must —" But here I broke down ; for Mrs. Brown, with the awful intuition of her sex, I saw at once was more occupied with my manner than my speech. So I tried a business *brusquerie*, and, placing the telegram in her hand, said hurriedly, "We must do something about this at once. It's perfectly absurd : but he will be here at one to-night. Beg thousand pardons ; but business prevented my speaking before"—and paused out of breath and courage.

Mrs. Brown read the telegram gravely, lifted her pretty eyebrows, turned the paper over, and looked on the other side, and then, in a remote and chilling voice, asked me if she understood me to say that the mother was coming also.

"Oh, dear, no ! " I exclaimed with considerable relief. "The mother is dead, you know. Sylvester, that is my friend who sent this, shot her when the baby was only three days old." But the expression of Mrs. Brown's face at this moment was so alarming, that I saw that nothing but the fullest explanation would save me. Hastily, and I fear not very coherently, I told her all.

She relaxed sweetly. She said I had frightened her with my talk about lions. Indeed, I think my picture of poor Baby, albeit a trifle highly coloured, touched her motherly heart. She was even a little vexed at what she called Sylvester's " hardhearted- ness." Still I was not without some apprehension. It was two months since I had seen him ; and Sylvester's vague allusion to his " slinging an ugly left" pained me. I looked at sympathetic little Mrs. Brown ; and the thought of Watson's pups covered me with guilty confusion.

Mrs. Brown had agreed to sit up with me until he arrived. One o'clock came, but no Baby. Two o'clock, three o'clock, passed. It was almost four when there was a wild clatter of horses' hoofs out- side, and with a jerk a waggon stopped at the door. In an instant I had opened it, and confronted a stranger. Almost at the same moment, the horses attempted to run away with the waggon.

The stranger's appearance was, to say the least, disconcerting. His clothes were badly torn and frayed ; his linen sack hung from his shoulders like a herald's apron ; one of his hands was bandaged ; his face scratched ; and there was no hat on his dishevelled head.   To add to the general effect, he had evidently sought relief from his woes in drink; and he swayed from side to side as he clung to the door-handle, and, in a very thick voice, stated that he had "suthin" for me outside.   When he had finished, the horses made another plunge.

Mrs. Brown thought they must be frightened at something.

"Frightened!" laughed the stranger, with bitter irony.   "Oh, no! Hossish ain't frightened? On'y ran away four timesh comin' here.   Oh, no! Nobody's frightened.   Every thin's all ari'.   Ain't it, Bill?" he said, addressing the driver.   "On'y been overboard twish; knocked down a hatchway once. Thash nothin'!   On'y two men unner doctor's han's at Stockton.   Thash nothin'!   Six hunner dollarsh cover all dammish."

I was too much disheartened to reply, but moved towards the waggon.   The stranger eyed me with an astonishment that almost sobered him.

"Do you reckon to tackle that animile yourself?" he asked, as he surveyed me from head to foot.

I did not speak, but, with an appearance of boldness I was far from feeling, walked to the waggon, and called "Baby!"

"All ri'.   Cash loose them straps, Bill, and stan' clear."

The straps were cut loose; and Baby, the remorseless, the terrible, quietly tumbled to the ground, and, rolling to my side, rubbed his foolish head against me.

I think the astonishment of the two men was beyond any vocal expression. Without a word, the drunken stranger got into the waggon, and drove away.

And Baby? He had grown, it is true, a trifle larger; but he was thin, and bore the marks of evident ill usage. His beautiful coat was matted and unkempt; and his claws, those bright steel hooks, had been ruthlessly pared to the quick. His eyes were furtive and restless; and the old expression of stupid good humour had changed to one of intelligent distrust. His intercourse with mankind had evidently quickened his intellect, without broadening his moral nature.

I had great difficulty in keeping Mrs. Brown from smothering him in blankets, and ruining his digestion with the delicacies of her larder; but I at last got him completely rolled up in the corner of my room, and asleep. I lay awake some time later with plans for his future. I finally determined to take him to Oakland—where I had built a little cottage, and always spent my Sundays—the very next day. And in the midst of a rosy picture of domestic felicity, I fell asleep.

When I awoke, it was broad day. My eyes at once sought the corner where Baby had been lying; but he was gone. I sprang from the bed, looked under it, searched the closet, but in vain. The door was still locked ; but there were the marks of his blunted claws upon the sill of the window that I had forgotten to close. He had evidently escaped that way. But where ? The window opened upon a balcony, to which the only other entrance was through the hall. He must be still in the house.

My hand was already upon the bell-rope ; but I stayed it in time. If he had not made himself known, why should I disturb the house ? I dressed myself hurriedly, and slipped into the hall. The first object that met my eyes was a boot lying upon the stairs. It bore the marks of Baby's teeth ; and, as I looked along the hall, I saw too plainly that the usual array of freshly-blackened boots and shoes before the lodgers' doors was not there. As I ascended the stairs, I found another, but with the blacking carefully licked off. On the third floor were two or three more boots, slightly mouthed ; but at this point Baby's taste for blacking had evidently palled. A little further on was a ladder leading to an open scuttle. I mounted the ladder, and reached the flat roof, that formed a continuous level over the row of houses to the corner of the street. Behind the chimney on the very last roof, something was lurking. It was the fugitive Baby. He was covered with dust and dirt and fragments of glass. But he was sitting on his hind-legs, and was eating an enormous slab of peanut candy, with a look of mingled guilt and infinite satisfaction. He even, I fancied, slightly stroked his stomach with his disengaged fore-paw as I approached. He knew that I was looking for him ; and the expression of his eye said plainly, " The past, at least, is secure."

I hurried him, with the evidences of his guilt, back to the scuttle, and descended on tiptoe to the floor beneath. Providence favoured us : I met no one on the stairs ; and his own cushioned tread was inaudible. I think he was conscious of the dangers of detection ; for he even forebore to breathe, or much less chew the last mouthful he had taken ; and he skulked at my side with the syrup dropping from his motionless jaws. I think he would have silently choked to death just then, for my sake ; and it was not until I had reached my room again, and threw myself panting on the sofa, that I saw how near strangulation he had been. He gulped once or twice apologetically, and then walked to the corner of his own accord, and rolled himself up like an immense sugarplum, sweating remorse and treacle at every pore.

I locked him in when I went to breakfast, when I found Mrs. Brown's lodgers in a state of intense excitement over certain mysterious events of the night before, and the dreadful revelations of the morning. It appeared that burglars had entered the block from the scuttles; that, being suddenly alarmed, they had quitted our house without committing any depredation, dropping even the boots they had collected in the halls ; but that a desperate attempt had been made to force the till in the confectioner's shop on the corner, and that the glass show-cases had been ruthlessly smashed.   A courageous servant in No. 4 had seen a masked burglar, on his hands and knees, attempting to enter their scuttle ; but, on her shouting, "Away wid yees !" he instantly fled.

I sat through this recital with cheeks that burned uncomfortably ; nor was I the less embarrassed, on raising my eyes, to meet Mrs. Brown's fixed curiously and mischievously on mine. As soon as I could make my escape from the table, I did so, and, running rapidly upstairs, sought refuge from any possible inquiry in my own room. Baby was still asleep in the corner. It would not be safe to remove him until the lodgers had gone down town; and I was revolving in my mind the expediency of keeping him until night veiled his obtrusive eccentricity from the public eye, when there came a cautious tap at my door. I opened it. Mrs. Brown slipped in quietly, closed the door softly, stood with her back against it, and her hand on the knob, and beckoned me mysteriously towards her. Then she asked in a low voice—

" Is hair-dye poisonous ? "

I was too confounded to speak.

"Oh, do! you know what I mean," she said impatiently. "This stuff." She produced suddenly from behind her a bottle with a Greek label, so

long as to run two or three times spirally round
it from top to bottom. "He says it isn't a dye:
it's a vegetable preparation, for invigorating—"

"Who says?" I asked, despairingly.

"Why, Mr. Parker, of course!" said Mrs. Brown,
severely, with the air of having repeated the name
a great many times—"the old gentleman in the
room above. The simple question I want to ask,"
she continued, with the calm manner of one who
has just convicted another of gross ambiguity of
language, "is only this: If some of this stuff were
put in a saucer, and left carelessly on the table,
and a child, a baby, or a cat, or any young animal,
should come in at the window, and drink it up—a
whole saucer full—because it had a sweet taste,
would it be likely to hurt them?"

I cast an anxious glance at Baby, sleeping peacefully in the corner, and a very grateful one at Mrs.
Brown, and said I didn't think it would.

"Because," said Mrs. Brown loftily, as she opened
the door, "I thought, if it was poisonous, remedies
might be used in time. Because," she added suddenly, abandoning her lofty manner, and wildly
rushing to the corner with a frantic embrace of the
unconscious Baby, "because, if any nasty stuff
should turn its booful hair a horrid green, or a
naughty pink, it would break its own muzzer's
heart, it would."

But, before I could assure Mrs. Brown of the in-
efficiency of hair-dye as an internal application,
she had darted from the room.

That night, with the secrecy of defaulters, Baby and I decamped from Mrs. Brown's. Distrusting the too emotional nature of that noble animal, the horse, I had recourse to a hand-cart, drawn by a stout Irishman, to convey my charge to the ferry. Even then, Baby refused to go unless I walked by the cart, and at times rode in it.

"I wish," said Mrs. Brown, as she stood by the door, wrapped in an immense shawl, and saw us depart, "I wish it looked less solemn—less like a pauper's funeral."

I must admit that, as I walked by the cart that night, I felt very much as if I were accompanying the remains of some humble friend to his last resting-place ; and that, when I was obliged to ride in it, I never could entirely convince myself that I was not helplessly overcome by liquor, or the victim of an accident, *en route* to the hospital. But at last we reached the ferry. On the boat, I think no one discovered Baby, except a drunken man, who approached me to ask for a light for his cigar, but who suddenly dropped it, and fled in dismay to the gentlemen's cabin, where his incoherent ravings were luckily taken for the earlier indications of *delirium tremens.*

It was nearly midnight when I reached my little cottage on the outskirts of Oakland ; and it was with a feeling of relief and security that I entered, locked the door, and turned him loose in the hall, satisfied that henceforth his depredations would be limited to my own property. He was very quiet that night; and after he had tried to mount the hat-rack, under the mistaken impression that it was intended for his own gymnastic exercise, and knocked all the hats off, he went peaceably to sleep on the rug.

In a week, with the exercise afforded him by the run of a large, carefully-boarded enclosure, he recovered his health, strength, spirits, and much of his former beauty. His presence was unknown to my neighbours, although it was noticeable that horses invariably "shied" in passing to the windward of my house, and that the baker and milkman had great difficulty in the delivery of their wares in the morning, and indulged in unseemly and unnecessary profanity in so doing.

At the end of the week, I determined to invite a few friends to see the Baby, and to that purpose wrote a number of formal invitations. After descanting, at some length, on the great expense and danger attending his capture and training, I offered a programme of the performance of the " Infant Phenomenon of Sierran Solitudes," drawn up into the highest professional profusion of alliteration and capital letters. A few extracts will give the reader some idea of his educational progress :—

1. He will, rolled up in a Round Ball, roll down the Wood-Shed Rapidly, illustrating His manner of Escaping from His Enemy in His Native Wilds.
2. He will Ascend the Well-Pole, and remove from the Very

L

Top a Hat, and as much of the Crown and Brim thereof, as May be Permitted.

3. He will perform in a pantomime, descriptive of the Conduct of The Big Bear, The Middle-sized Bear, and The Little Bear of the Popular Nursery Legend.

4. He will shake his chain Rapidly, showing his Manner of striking Dismay and Terror in the Breasts of Wanderers in Ursine Wildernesses.

The morning of the exhibition came; but an hour before the performance the wretched Baby was missing. The Chinese cook could not indicate his whereabouts. I searched the premises thoroughly; and then, in despair, took my hat, and hurried out into the narrow lane that led towards the open fields and the woods beyond. But I found no trace nor track of Baby Sylvester. I returned, after an hour's fruitless search, to find my guests already assembled on the rear veranda. I briefly recounted my disappointment, my probable loss, and begged their assistance.

"Why," said a Spanish friend, who prided himself on his accurate knowledge of English, to Barker, who seemed to be trying vainly to rise from his reclining position on the veranda, "why do you not disengage yourself from the veranda of our friend? And why, in the name of Heaven, do you attach to yourself so much of this thing, and make to yourself such unnecessary contortion? Ah," he continued, suddenly withdrawing one of his own feet from the veranda with an evident effort, "I am myself attached! Surely it is something here!"

It evidently was. My guests were all rising with difficulty. The floor of the veranda was covered with some glutinous substance. It was—syrup!

I saw it all in a flash. I ran to the barn. The keg of "golden syrup," purchased only the day before, lay empty upon the floor. There were sticky tracks all over the enclosure, but still no Baby.

"There's something moving the ground over there by that pile of dirt," said Barker.

He was right. The earth was shaking in one corner of the enclosure like an earthquake. I approached cautiously. I saw, what I had not before noticed, that the ground was thrown up; and there, in the middle of an immense grave-like cavity, crouched Baby Sylvester, still digging, and slowly but surely sinking from sight in a mass of dust and clay.

What were his intentions? Whether he was stung by remorse, and wished to hide himself from my reproachful eyes, or whether he was simply trying to dry his syrup-besmeared coat, I never shall know; for that day, alas! was his last with me.

He was pumped upon for two hours, at the end of which time he still yielded a thin treacle. He was then taken and carefully inwrapped in blankets, and locked up in the store-room. The next morning he was gone! The lower portion of the window sash and pane were gone too. His successful experiments on the fragile texture of glass at the confectioner's, on the first day of his entrance to civilization, had not been lost upon him. His first essay at combining cause and effect ended in his escape.

Where he went, where he hid, who captured him, if he did not succeed in reaching the foot hills beyond Oakland, even the offer of a large reward, backed by the efforts of an intelligent police, could not discover. I never saw him again from that day until——

Did I see him? I was in a horse-car on Sixth Avenue, a few days ago, when the horses suddenly became unmanageable, and left the track for the sidewalk, amid the oaths and execrations of the driver. Immediately in front of the car a crowd had gathered around two performing bears and a showman. One of the animals, thin, emaciated, and the mere wreck of his native strength, attracted my attention. I endeavoured to attract his. He turned a pair of bleared, sightless eyes in my direction; but there was no sign of recognition. I leaned from the car-window, and called softly, "Baby!" But he did not heed. I closed the window. The car was just moving on, when he suddenly turned, and, either by accident or design, thrust a callous paw through the glass.

"It's worth a dollar and a half to put in a new pane," said the conductor; "if folks will play with bears!——."

A JERSEY CENTENARIAN.

I HAVE seen her at last. She is a hundred and seven years old, and remembers George Washington quite distinctly. It is somewhat confusing, however, that she also remembers a contemporaneous Josiah W. Perkins, of Basking Ridge, N.J., and, I think, has the impression that Perkins was the better man. Perkins, at the close of the last century, paid her some little attention. There are a few things that a really noble woman of a hundred and seven never forgets.

It was Perkins who said to her in 1795, in the streets of Philadelphia, "Shall I show thee Gen. Washington?" Then she said, careless-like (for you know, child, at that time it wasn't what it is now to see Gen. Washington), she said, "So do, Josiah, so do!" Then he pointed to a tall man who got out of a carriage, and went into a large house. He was larger than you be. He wore his own hair—not powdered; had a flowered chintz vest, with yellow breeches and blue stockings, and a broad-brimmed hat. In summer he wore a white straw hat, and at his farm at Basking Ridge he always wore it: At this point, it became too evident that she was describing the clothes of the all fascinating Perkins : so I gently but firmly led her back to Washington. Then it appeared that she did not remember exactly what he wore. To assist her, I sketched the general historic dress of that period. She said she thought he was dressed like that. Emboldened by my success, I added a hat of Charles II., and pointed shoes of the eleventh century. She endorsed these with such cheerful alacrity that I dropped the subject.

The house upon which I had stumbled, or, rather, to which my horse—a Jersey hack, accustomed to historic researches—had brought me, was low and quaint. Like most old houses, it had the appearance of being encroached upon by the surrounding glebe, as if it were already half in the grave, with a sod or two, in the shape of moss thrown on it, like ashes on ashes, and dust on dust. A wooden house, instead of acquiring dignity with age, is apt to lose its youth and respectability together. A porch, with scant, sloping seats, from which even the winter's snow must have slid uncomfortably, projected from a doorway that opened most unjustifiably into a small sitting-room. There was no vestibule, or *locus pœnitentiæ*, for the embarrassed or bashful visitor : he passed at once from the security of the public road into shameful privacy. And here, in the mellow autumnal sunlight, that, streaming through the maples and sumach on the opposite bank, flickered and danced upon the floor, she sat and discoursed of George Washington,

and thought of Perkins. She was quite in keeping
with the house and the season, albeit a little in
advance of both ; her skin being of a faded russet,
and her hands so like dead November leaves
that I fancied they even rustled when she moved
them.

For all that, she was quite bright and cheery ;
her faculties still quite vigorous, although performing irregularly and spasmodically. It was somewhat discomposing, I confess, to observe that at
times her lower jaw would drop, leaving her speech-
less, until one of the family would notice it, and
raise it smartly into place with a slight snap—an
operation always performed in such an habitual,
perfunctory manner, generally in passing to and
fro in their household duties, that it was very trying
to the spectator. It was still more embarrassing
to observe that the dear old lady had evidently no
knowledge of this, but believed she was still talking,
and that, on resuming her actual vocal utterance,
she was often abrupt and incoherent, beginning
always in the middle of a sentence, and often in the
middle of a word. " Sometimes," said her daughter,
a giddy, thoughtless young thing of eighty-five—
" sometimes just moving her head sort of unhitches
her jaw ; and, if we don't happen to see it, she'll go
on talking for hours without ever making a sound."
Although I was convinced, after this, that during my
interview I had lost several important revelations regarding George Washington through these peculiar

lapses, I could not help reflecting how beneficent were these provisions of the Creator,—how, if properly studied and applied, they might be fraught with happiness to mankind—how a slight jostle or jar at a dinner-party might make the post-prandial eloquence of garrulous senility satisfactory to itself yet harmless to others—how a more intimate knowlege of anatomy, introduced into the domestic circle, might make a home tolerable at least, if not happy—how a long-suffering husband, under the pretence of a conjugal caress, might so unhook his wife's condyloid process as to allow the flow of expostulation, criticism, or denunciation to go on with gratification to her, and perfect immunity to himself.

But this was not getting back to George Washington and the early struggles of the Republic. So I returned to the commander-in-chief, but found, after one or two leading questions, that she was rather inclined to resent his re-appearance on the stage. Her reminiscences here were chiefly social and local, and more or less flavoured with Perkins. We got back as far as the Revolutionary epoch, or, rather, her impressions of that epoch, when it was still fresh in the public mind. And here I came upon an incident, purely personal and local, but, withal, so novel, weird, and uncanny, that for a while I fear it quite displaced George Washington in my mind, and tinged the autumnal fields beyond with a red that was not of the sumach:

I do not remember to have read of it in the books. I do not know that it is entirely authentic. It was attested to me by mother and daughter as an uncontradicted tradition.

In the little field beyond, where the plough still turns up musket-balls and cartridge-boxes, took place one of those irregular skirmishes between the militiamen and Knyphausen's stragglers, that made the retreat historical. A Hessian soldier, wounded in both legs and utterly helpless, dragged himself to the cover of a hazel-copse, and lay there hidden for two days. On the third day, maddened by thirst, he managed to creep to the rail-fence of an adjoining farm-house, but found himself unable to mount it or pass through. There was no one in the house but a little girl of six or seven years. He called to her, and in a faint voice asked for water. She returned to the house, as if to comply with his request, but, mounting a chair, took from the chimney a heavily-loaded Queen Anne musket, and, going to the door, took aim at the helpless intruder, and fired. The man fell back dead, without a groan. She replaced the musket, and, returning to the fence, covered the body with boughs and leaves, until it was hidden. Two or three days after, she related the occurrence in a careless, casual way, and leading the way to the fence, with a piece of bread and butter in her guileless fingers, pointed out the result of her simple, unsophisticated effort. The Hessian was decently buried,

but I could not find out what became of the little
girl.   Nobody seemed to remember.   I trust that,
in after years, she was happily married ; that no
Jersey Lovelace attempted to trifle with a heart
whose impulses were so prompt, and whose pur-
poses were so sincere.   They did not seem to know
if she had married or not.   Yet it does not seem
probable that such simplicity of conception, frankness of expression, and deftness of execution were
lost to posterity, or that they failed, in their time
and season, to give flavour to the domestic felicity
of the period.   Beyond this, the story perhaps has
little value, except as an offset to the usual anec-
dotes of Hessian atrocity.

They had their financial panics even in Jersey,
in the old days.   She remembered when Dr. White
married your cousin Mary—or was it Susan ?—yes,
it was Susan.   She remembers that your Uncle
Harry brought in an armful of bank-notes—paper
money, you know—and threw them in the corner,
saying they were no good to anybody.   She remembered playing with them, and giving them to
your Aunt Anna—no, child, it was your own
mother, bless your heart !   Some of them was
marked as high as a hundred dollars.   Everybody
kept gold and silver in a stocking, or in a " chaney "
vase, like that.   You never used money to buy anything.   When Josiah went to Springfield to buy anything, he took a cartload of things with him to ex-
change.   That yaller picture-frame was paid for in

greenings. But then people knew just what they had. They didn't fritter their substance away in unchristian trifles, like your father, Eliza Jane, who doesn't know that there is a God who will smite him hip and thigh ; for vengeance is mine, and those that believe in me. But here, singularly enough, the inferior maxillaries gave out, and her jaw dropped. (I noticed that her giddy daughter of eighty-five was sitting near her ; but I do not pretend to connect this fact with the arrested flow of personal disclosure.) Howbeit, when she re-covered her speech again, it appeared that she was complaining of the weather.

The seasons had changed very much since your father went to sea. The winters used to be terrible in those days. When she went over to Springfield, in June, she saw the snow still on Watson's Ridge. There were whole days when you couldn't git over to William Henry's, their next neighbour, a quarter of a mile away. It was that dreful winter that the Spanish sailor was found. You don't remember the Spanish sailor, Eliza Jane—it was before your time. There was a little personal skirmishing here, which I feared, at first, might end in a suspension of maxillary functions, and the loss of the story ; but here it is. Ah, me ! it is a pure white winter idyl : how shall I sing it this bright, gay autumnal day ?

It was a terrible night, that winter's night, when she and the century were young together. The sun was lost at three o'clock : the snowy night came down like a white sheet, that flapped around the house, beat at the windows with its edges, and at last wrapped it in a close embrace. In the middle of the night, they thought they heard above the wind a voice crying "Christus, Christus!" in a foreign tongue. They opened the door—no easy task in the north wind that pressed its strong shoulders against it—but nothing was to be seen but the drifting snow. The next morning dawned on fences hidden, and a landscape changed and obliterated with drift. During the day, they again heard the cry of "Christus!" this time faint and hidden, like a child's voice. They searched in vain : the drifted snow hid its secret. On the third day they broke a path to the fence, and then they heard the cry distinctly. Digging down, they found the body of a man—a Spanish sailor, dark and bearded, with ear-rings in his ears. As they stood gazing down at his cold and pulseless figure, the cry of "Christus!" again rose upon the wintry air; and they turned and fled in superstitious terror to the house. And then one of the children, bolder than the rest, knelt down, and opened the dead man's rough pea-jacket, and found—what think you ?—a little blue and green parrot, nestling against his breast. It was the bird that had echoed mechanically the last despairing cry of the life that was given to save it. It was the bird that ever after, amid outlandish oaths and wilder sailor-songs, that I fear often shocked the pure ears of its gentle mistress, and brought scandal into the Jerseys, still retained that one weird and mournful cry.

The sun meanwhile was sinking behind the steadfast range beyond, and I could not help feeling that I must depart with my wants unsatisfied. I had brought away no historic fragment: I absolutely knew little or nothing new regarding George Washington. I had been addressed variously by the names of different members of the family who were dead and forgotten ; I had stood for an hour in the past : yet I had not added to my historical knowledge, nor the practical benefit of your readers. I spoke once more of Washington, and she replied with a reminiscence of Perkins.

Stand forth, O Josiah W. Perkins, of Basking Ridge, N. J. Thou wast of little account in thy life, I warrant ; thou didst not even feel the greatness of thy day and time ; thou didst criticise thy superiors ; thou wast small and narrow in thy ways ; thy very name and grave are unknown and uncared for : but thou wast once kind to a woman who survived thee, and, lo ! thy name is again spoken of men, and for a moment lifted up above thy betters.

J. OGDEN AND CO., PRINTERS, 172, ST. JOHN STREET, E.C.

Paper Covers.	Limp Cl. Gilt.		Picture Boards.	Cloth.
		LEVER, Charles—		
—	—	Arthur O'Leary	2/	2/6
—	—	Con Cregan	2/	2/6
		LE FANU, Sheridan—		
—	—	Torlogh O'Brien	2/	—
		LONG, Lady Catherine—		
—	—	Sir Roland Ashton	2/	2/6
		LOVER, Samuel—		
—	—	Handy Andy	2/	2/6
—	—	Rory O'More	2/	2/6
		LYTTON, Right Hon. Lord—		
—	—	Alice : Sequel to Ernest Maltravers	2/	2/6
—	—	Caxtons	2/	2/6
—	—	Coming Race	2/	2/6
—	—	Devereux	2/	2/6
—	—	Disowned	2/	2/6
—	—	Ernest Maltravers	2/	2/6
—	—	Eugene Aram	2/	2/6
—	—	Godolphin	2/	2/6
—	—	Harold	2/	2/6
—	—	The Last of the Barons	2/	2/6
—	—	Leila		
—	—	The Pilgrims of the Rhine ..	2/	2/6
—	—	Lucretia	2/	2/6
—	—	My Novel, vol. 1	2/	2/6
—	—	Do. vol. 2	2/	2/6
—	—	Night and Morning	2/	2/6
—	—	Paul Clifford	2/	2/6
—	—	Pelham	2/	2/6
—	—	Pompeii, The Last Days of ...	2/	2/6
—	—	Rienzi	2/	2/6
—	—	Strange Story	2/	2/6
—	·-	What will He Do with It? vol. 1 ...	2/	2/6
—	—	Do. do. vol. 2 ...	2/	2/6
—	⊤	Zanoni	2/	2/6

Sets of Lord Lytton's Novels, 22 vols., fcap. 8vo, cloth, £2 15s.;
boards, £2 4s. (*See also page 18.*)

(*See also page 18.*)

		MAILLARD, Mrs.—		
1/	-	Adrien	—	—
1/	—	Compulsory Marriage ·... ...	—	—
1/	—	Zingra the Gipsy	—	—

Paper Covers.	Limp Cl. Gilt.		Picture Boards.	Half Roan.
		MAXWELL, W. H.—		
—	—	The Bivouac	2/	2/6
—	—	Brian O'Linn ; or, Luck is Every-		
		thing	2/	2/6
—	—	Captain Blake ; or, My Life ...	2/	2/6
—	—	Captain O'Sullivan	2/	2/6
—	—	Flood and Field	2/	2/6
—	—	Hector O'Halloran	2/	2/6
—	—	Stories of the Peninsular War ...	2/	2/6
1/	—	Stories of Waterloo	2/	2/6
—	—	Wild Sports in the Highlands ...	2/	2/6
—	—	Wild Sports in the West	2/	2/6

The Set, in 10 vols., half roan, £1 5s.

MARK TWAIN—

(*See* "AMERICAN LIBRARY," *page* 24.)

MARRYAT, Captain—

(*See also pages* 19, 20.) Cl. Gilt.

Paper Covers.	Limp Cl. Gilt.		Picture Boards.	Cl. Gilt.
1/	1/6	Dog Fiend	2/	2/6
1/	1/6	Frank Mildmay	2/	2/6
1/	1/6	Jacob Faithful	2/	2/6
1/	1/6	Japhet in Search of a Father ...	2/	2/6
1/	1/6	King's Own	2/	2/6
1/	1/6	Midshipman Easy	2	2/6
1/	1/6	Monsieur Violet	-	—
1/	1/6	Newton Forster	2/	2/6
1/	1/6	Olla Podrida	—	—
1/	1/6	Percival Keene	2/	2/6
1/	1/6	Phantom Ship	2/	2/6
1/	1/6	Poacher	2/	2/6
1/	1/6	Pacha of Many Tales	2/	2/6
1/	1/6	Peter Simple	2/	2/6
1/	1/6	Rattlin the Reefer	2/	2/6
1/	1/6	Valerie	—	—

The Set of Captain Marryat's Novels, 16 vols. bound in 8, cloth, £1 5s. ; 16 vols, cloth, £1 ; paper, 16s. ; 13 vols. (Steel Plates), cloth, £1 12s. 6d.

MARTINEAU, Harriet— Hf. Roan.

Paper Covers.	Limp Cl. Gilt.		Picture Boards.	Half Roan.
-	—	The Hour and the Man	2/	2/6

NOVELS AT ONE SHILLING.

W. H. AINSWORTH.

Windsor Castle.
The Tower of London.
The Miser's Daughter.
Rookwood.
Old St. Paul's.
Crichton.
Guy Fawkes.
The Spendthrift.
James the Second.
The Star Chamber.
The Flitch of Bacon.
Lancashire Witches.
Mervyn Clitheroe.
Ovingdean Grange.
St. James's.
Auriol.
Jack Sheppard.

WM. CARLETON.

Jane Sinclair.
The Clarionet.
The Tithe Proctor.
Fardarougha.
The Emigrants.

J. FENIMORE COOPER.

The Pilot.
Last of the Mohicans.
The Pioneers.
The Red Rover.
The Spy.
Lionel Lincoln.
The Deerslayer.
The Pathfinder.
The Bravo.
The Waterwitch.
Two Admirals.
Satanstoe.
Afloat and Ashore.
Wyandotte.
Eve Effingham.
Miles Wallingford.
The Headsman.
The Prairie.
Homeward Bound.
The Borderers.

The Sea Lions.
Precaution.
The Oak Openings.
Mark's Reef.
Ned Myers.
Heidenmauer.

CHARLES DICKENS.

Sketches by Boz.
The Pickwick Papers.
Oliver Twist.
Nicholas Nickleby.

ALEXANDRE DUMAS.

The Three Musketeers.
Twenty Years After.
Dr. Basilius.
The Twin Captains.
Captain Paul.
Memoirs of a Physician.
  2 vols. (1s. each.)
The Chevalier de Maison Rouge.
The Queen's Necklace.
Countess de Charny.
Monte Cristo, 2 vols.
  (1s. each.)
Nanon.
The Two Dianas.
The Black Tulip.
The Forty-five Guardsmen.
The Taking of the Bastile, 2 vols. (1s. each.)
Chicot, the Jester.
The Conspirators.
Ascanio.
Page of Duke of Savoy.
Isabel of Bavaria.
Beau Tancrede.
The Regent's Daughter.
Pauline.
Catherine Blum.
The Ingènue.
The Russian Gipsy.
The Watchmaker.
The Corsican Brothers.

GERALD GRIFFIN.

The Munster Festivals.
The Rivals.
The Colleen Bawn.

NATH. HAWTHORNE.

The Scarlet Letter.
House of Seven Gables.
Mosses from an Old Manse.

Lord LYTTON.

Kenelm Chillingly.
The Parisians, 2 vols.
Falkland and Zicci.
Pelham.
Paul Clifford.
Eugene Aram.
Rienzi.
Leila, and The Pilgrims of the Rhine.
The Last of the Barons.
Ernest Maltravers.
Godolphin.
The Disowned.
Devereux.

Capt. MARRYAT.

Peter Simple.
The King's Own.
Midshipman Easy.
Rattlin the Reefer.
Pacha of Many Tales.
Newton Forster.
Jacob Faithful.
The Dog Fiend.
Japhet in Search of a Father.
The Poacher.
The Phantom Ship.
Percival Keene.
Valerie.
Frank Mildmay.
Olla Podrida.
Monsieur Violet.
The Pirate, and The Three Cutters.

VARIOUS AUTHORS.

Julie de Bourg.
Lilias Davenant.
The Soldier of Fortune.   STEWART.
Compulsory Marriage.   CURLING.
Stories of Waterloo.   MAILLARD.
The Divorced.   MAXWELL.
The Albatross.   Lady C. BURY.
Cinq Mars.   KINGSTON.
Zingra, the Gipsy.   DE VIGNY.
The Little Wife.   MAILLARD.
Adelaide Lindsay.   Mrs. GREY.
" Emilia Wyndham."   By Author of
A Family Feud.   T. COOPER.
Tom Jones.   FIELDING.
A Week with Mossoo.   C. ROSS.

Out for a Holiday with Cook.
    SKETCHLEY.
Tristram Shandy, and A Sentimental Journey.   STERNE.
The Mountaineer of the Atlas.
    W. S. MAYO.
The Mysteries of Udolpho. Complete Edition.   Mrs RADCLIFFE.
Log of the "Water Lily" during Three Cruises.
Through the Keyhole. J. M. JEPHSON.
King Dobbs.   JAMES HANNAY.
Fairy Water.
    Author of "George Geith."
The Hobbses and Dobbses.

GEORGE ROUTLEDGE & SONS.

4